Amos Oz

TOUCH THE WATER, TOUCH THE WIND

TRANSLATED FROM THE HEBREW BY
Nicholas de Lange

VINTAGE

Published by Vintage 2004

2 4 6 8 10 9 7 5 3 1

Copyright © Amos Oz 1973
English translation copyright © Chatto & Windus
and Harcourt Brace Jovanovich Inc, 1974

Amos Oz has asserted his right under the Copyright, Designs
and Patents Act, 1988 to be identified as the author of
this work

First published in Great Britain in 1975 by
Chatto & Windus

Vintage
Random House, 20 Vauxhall Bridge Road,
London SW1V 2SA

Random House Australia (Pty) Limited
20 Alfred Street, Milsons Point, Sydney
New South Wales 2061, Australia

Random House New Zealand Limited
18 Poland Road, Glenfield,
Auckland 10, New Zealand

Random House (Pty) Limited
Endulini, 5A Jubilee Road, Parktown 2193,
South Africa

The Random House Group Limited Reg. No. 954009
www.randomhouse.co.uk/vintage

A CIP catalogue record for this book
is available from the British Library

ISBN 0 09 981750 0

Papers used by Random House are natural, recyclable
products made from wood grown in sustainable forests.
The manufacturing processes conform to the environ-
mental regulations of the country of origin

Printed and bound in Denmark by
AIT Nørhaven, Viborg

Poland. Early winter. 1939.

A Jewish schoolmaster by the name of Pomeranz had fled from the Germans and gone into hiding in the forest. He was a short man with tiny eyes and thick, vicious jaws. He looked like a spy in an American comedy.

He was a teacher of mathematics and physics in the Mickiewicz National Gymnasium in the town of M——. His spare hours were given over to some kind of theoretical research; the secrets of Nature aroused a powerful passion in him. Rumour had it that he was on the verge of producing a discovery in the field of electricity or magnetism. And above his upper lip he lovingly cultivated a thin, nervous moustache.

At first Pomeranz hid in the depths of the forest in a deserted hut which had belonged to a woodcutter named Dziobak Przywolski. This Przywolski had been killed the previous spring by the peasants. They had chopped him to death with an axe because he always walked about the forest wearing an orange pointed hat and red boots, casually performed small wonders in front of the villagers, and claimed to have been born of a virgin. Among other things he had the power of healing an aching tooth by means of spells, of seducing a young peasant girl with the help of liturgical chants, of rousing the shepherd dogs to mad barking and then calming them down with a wave of the hand, and of levitating slightly at night, if only the wind was right. He was also in the habit of belching, and of stealing chickens left and right.

One Good Friday the woodcutter boasted to the peasants that if they hit him with all their might with his axe the axe would break. So they hit him, and the axe did not break.

Pomeranz sat alone in the abandoned hut, contemplating the gradual disintegration of the roof beams, listening with strained ears to the restlessness of the forest at night, to the savage wind lashing the cowering tree-tops, to the whispering sadness of leaves.

He was left to himself day and night. He thought about many different things.

Far off down the forest slopes, where the undergrowth lapped at the river, German engineers dynamited all the railway bridges. Because of the murky distance and the thick moist air there was a delay, a hesitation almost, between the flash of each explosion and the low rumble of thunder. This delay, momentary though it was, gave an almost comical appearance to the whole spectacle, so that Pomeranz in his hideout was assailed by doubts. And, indeed, a few days later, on receipt of fresh orders, the same engineers reappeared, in the grip of a fever-ish enthusiasm, and began measuring the river and furiously rebuilding everything as it had been before; they stretched steel cables, planted concrete piles, erected a pair of twin prefabricated bridges, and restored everything to its former state.

But once again the distance and the autumn light bestowed an unreal, almost absurd, character on the frantic activity at the foot of the slope: tiny human figures, voices losing themselves among the hills, and the patient grey skyline. Time and again at evening melancholy forces landed and overran the forests and hills with dull, murky darkness.

Bread and water were provided him by an old sorceress from the village.

Terrified peasants would approach on tiptoe, occasionally depositing a roast goose at a safe distance from the hut, and vanishing instantly into the bosom of the

6

forest. Dziobak Przywolski, the belching son of a virgin, had warned them in advance that he would soon return in another guise.

Or perhaps there were no peasants and no sorceress, and no roast geese, but Pomeranz lived there in a state of pure spirit, lacking all physical needs.

2

Stefa Pomeranz did not go into hiding in the forest with her husband, but stayed behind in her home in the town of M——. She taught German thought in the same Mickiewicz Gymnasium, and even maintained a postal and telepathic correspondence with Martin Heidegger, the famous philosopher.

She was not in the least apprehensive of the Germans. In the first place, she abhorred wars, et cetera, and had no faith in them. Secondly, from the racial point of view she was only Jewish up to a point, and in outlook she was a devoted European. Moreover, she was a fully paid-up member of the Goethe Society.

Stefa stayed alone all day long in her artistically furnished little apartment, where she spent a few hours each day preparing the latest studies of Professor Zaicek for publication. Outside, disturbing things happened: Pomeranz ran away, Poland collapsed, German planes bombed the factories to the south, the railway repair sheds, and the army barracks, armoured cars streamed down Jaroslaw Avenue all night, at dawn flags were changed, and Stefa closed every single shutter in the house in disgust, and the windows too.

Long and lean on the sideboard in her study stood an African warrior carved in wood and covered in war paint. The warrior seemed poised to spring at a dainty pink nude girl in a Matisse painting on the wall opposite,

7

threatening her night and day with his huge fierce manhood.

Two ancient Siamese cats, Chopin and Schopenhauer, kept Stefa company. They slept curled up together on the rug in front of the open fire, filling the apartment with calm and tenderness. Sometimes Stefa thought she heard Pomeranz's slippered footsteps in the hall and his low cough, and once in the early hours of the morning her name was distinctly whispered. Here were his shaving things, here was his dressing gown, a smell of tobacco, a reminder of his silence. Everywhere there reigned an aggressive, uncompromising cleanness, shining kitchen and gleaming bathroom, tidy shelves and sparkling chandeliers. Stefa stayed alone all these days, behind her closed shutters. Gradually the apartment filled with a faint smell of perfume. From the picture rail, high above the piano and the many vases of flowers, a menacing bear's head stared down glassy-eyed at the sleeping Siamese cats.

The bear's expression was one of patient irony, verging on ultimate tranquillity.

Stefa was a beautiful, proud woman. From her youth on, all the local intelligentsia had wooed her with ideas and literature. Such an intelligent, artistic young lady, they had said, and now in a fit of caprice she suddenly gives herself to the dreamy son of a simple watchmaker. Such whims, they said, always die away as quickly as they are born. And the very name Pomeranz is absurdly incongruous for Stefa.

And indeed, when the Germans began to surround the town of M——, the dreamy son of a watchmaker fled alone to the forest, abandoning Stefa to her admirers, the local intelligentsia.

She hoped that he would succeed in surviving the present events and that she would see him again someday. She did not want to call her feelings by one name

8

or another, but she sighed for him and had great faith in his powers.

Night by night the German guards made shooting sounds in the distance. The electricity was subject to frequent interruptions. The tradesmen became noticeably slacker. The dustman and postman neglected their duties. The drunken gardener, who was nicknamed by everybody 'Run-Jesus,' suddenly without asking permission took to living in the woodshed at the bottom of the garden, insolence and a secret menace flashing in his eyes. He grinned, flattered, spoke a lot, came and went as he pleased. And the maid, Martha Pinch-me-not, as suddenly abandoned poor Professor Zaicek, in whose house she had worked for the past seven years. She was criticized by everyone, and there were those who saw in her move a bad omen for the future. Professor Zaicek, the pride of the city, was an elderly widowed scholar, whose name was well known all over Europe. He possessed a Karl Marx face deeply scored by suffering and wisdom.

The military governor of the town, a certain Baron Joachim von Topf, issued an edict : the army was compelled to requisition the Gymnasium buildings. For the time being all classes were cancelled. The Baron saw fit to append to the edict a word of apology to the citizens : the hardships of war-time would soon be over, and before long a new order would be established.

But the difficulties increased. The streetcars stopped running, prices soared, and the ancient belfry of St Stephen's Church – an architectural gem in Florentine style—was damaged by a stray bomb. Nightly the sound of bricks was heard clattering in the ruined church. Sometimes the falling bricks struck the bell at night, giving rise to numerous superstitious rumours. Even in the circles of the Catholic intelligentsia the view was expressed that everything was possible.

Various people, including some eminent citizens, abandoned the city. In the middle of Jaroslaw Avenue stood a burned-out streetcar, and a chestnut tree lay uprooted for several weeks. Professor Zaicek several times complained to intimate friends of an acute inflammation of the bladder. Grim and even wild rumours spread: women in the marketplace said that poor Jews, or priests, or perhaps only consumptives, were being transferred elsewhere by the authorities. The rumours were virtually impossible to trace, verify, or substantiate. In back alleys petty speculators proliferated nauseatingly. Even the library was temporarily closed.

Stefa was smitten by a secret disappointment. The war, for all its horrors and its vulgarity, had offered a certain possibility of rejuvenating Europe, of refreshing worn-out ideas, and of being a participating observer of a mighty historical event, but in fact on all sides there was nothing but drabness and pettiness. One night some drunken soldiers smashed the historic stained-glass windows of the Concert Hall. The statue of Adam Mickiewicz was defaced with a thin moustache which bore a remarkable resemblance to that of the vanished teacher of physics and mathematics; unruly soldiers, or schoolboys who had run riot in the night. On the corner of Magdalen Lane a Swabian corporal addressed Stefa in such illiterate German that she was appalled. Suddenly it dawned: time was running out. Stefa had never been very strong; she suffered from migraines in the morning.

Worst of all, postal communications with the outside world were rapidly deteriorating. The old stamps were withdrawn from circulation. Pianos were requisitioned from several houses. The new order tarried in coming. Over all, with sly tranquillity, the bear's glass eyes looked down. And from the grocers' shops Portuguese sardines vanished as if they had never existed.

3

Early in 1940, with the first breaths of a bizarrely
out-of-place spring, Pomeranz sallied forth from the hut
in which he had hidden all through the winter and
began to move from place to place. He assumed by
turns the various garbs of herdsman and railwayman,
peasant and priest. Gently, pensively, he glided south,
southwest, and south again, a slow, almost bashful
caressing movement across the dense forests. When the
hunt was near he hid all day in barns on the outskirts
of God-forsaken villages. At the onset of dusk he would
leave his hiding-place and stand lean and erect in the
darkness until he was cloaked in night, and then he
would play softly on a mouth organ. The Polish air
was instantly saturated with music. Pomeranz pawed the
muddy ground, gathered an inner momentum, belched,
sweated, leaned his elbows on the music he had discharged round about him, flailed with his arms, struggled
and pulled, got the wind behind him, and finally uttered
a soft grunt and wrenched himself free from the grip
of gravity.

He rose and floated on the dark air, his body slack
after the effort, borne high and silent over woods and
meadows, over churches, huts, and fields.

So he overcame all the obstacles in his way.

He had once learned, perhaps from his wife, that time
is subjective, an affection of the mind. And so he had
a low opinion of it.

Even material objects, if you plumb their depths, are
no more than vague images. In brief : ideas cannot be
perceived, and perceptible objects can never be grasped
by thought.

Ergo, nothing exists.

Germans, forests, huts, ghosts, wolves, dawn-stench of villages, haystacks, vampires, muddy streams, snowy expanses, all seemed to him a clumsy, ephemeral convergence of abstract energies. Even his own body appeared to him to be a wilful tide of transient energy.

As he passed his frostbitten fingers across his brow he suddenly seemed to touch a star. Or as he clasped his frozen legs together in the snow in the forest at night he seemed to be struggling to reconcile two opposing ideas. He learned to devour whole marrows and pumpkins and follow them with raw mushrooms.

Yet he spared the music, and for the time being refrained from reducing it to its mathematical structure. He was saving this possibility for a moment of despair, a last resort, an ultimate weapon. In the same way he dispelled the memory of his wife and his home : longing was a poisoned snare, a lethal dart. Throughout his journey he kept in his pocket a little mouth organ. He could rise in the air, soar high into the night, even discard his body, by means of a change of tune. And into his worn red boots he stuffed sackcloth against the biting cold.

Solitude and wandering trained this educated Jew to eat raw potatoes, to quench his thirst with handfuls of snow, to mislead the noses of old wolves, to plant his footprints backward in the snow to baffle all pursuit. He had the power of feeling his way, using his thoughts like radar beams, through the tangled network of forest paths. So he eluded the German guards and bands of partisans, avoided minefields and trip wires, made his circuitous way along the valleys among hostile villages, untouched by foxes, vampires, or villagers with axes. And in his tattered sleeve he carried a grubby certificate of baptism in the name of Dziobak Przywolski, son of Mary.

If suffering got the better of him, he would forget his pride and emerge at dusk from the forest darkness, aided by the long shadows and deceptive twilight, scare

a solitary peasant woman and plunder a goose or some
eggs or a woollen kerchief. These forest regions, cursed
by damp and darkness, were unloving and unloved.
Closing in on all sides, offering no escape. So he passed
on from darkness to darkness as if he too were cloaked
in darkness.

4

Days and nights passed, and his foot became painfully
inflamed. Melancholy overcame him, or perhaps for a
moment he was carried away by longing. In one of the
caves he lost his seven-league boots, or his hood of
invisibility fell apart. In short, the music died away
and the dreamy son of a watchmaker grew weaker and
weaker until he was captured by a German patrol.

A lame, rotund major with rimless spectacles took the
certificate of baptism from the prisoner and studied it
so thoroughly that the writing grew faint. Then he raised
a single, narrow eyebrow and ordered the short Son
of Mary to be taken to the cells : the brow, the vicious
eyes, the heavy jaws, his smell, and that insolent moustache, the expression of a spy in a comic film, and on
top of all the torn robe of an itinerant priest, everything
about him was obviously suspicious. Furthermore, the
boredom and the fleas were playing havoc with the
major and his men.

The cell was nothing more than the filthy cellar of an
abandoned monastery or seminary : crosses and obscene
drawings covered the walls. And the cold was piercing
and tormenting.

Pomeranz suddenly recalled a conversation which had
taken place years before. Stefa had taken him to the
Philosophical Soirée of the Goethe Society. The intelligentsia of the town of M—— were involved in a dis-

cussion of political vis-à-vis metaphysical wrong. Bright, bespectacled young men, all of them thin, gazed covertly at Stefa's legs, then at her plain, silent husband, and back again at her long-lashed eyes. Dream-stricken Stefa. When the first exchange of witticisms had died down, Professor Zaicek spoke about conflicting ideas and their universal tendency to circularity. His Karl Marx face silently radiated, as always, an agonized wisdom, and his voice when he spoke was tender and tired. Eventually they drank tea and nibbled cakes, and in the small hours of the morning they beguiled Stefa into playing some sad études, while they all gazed at her waist with moist eyes.

In the afternoon Pomeranz was brought up out of the cellar and interrogated tediously and offhandedly : where, when, why, what he had seen, about the potato crop in the Poznan region and the fish in the Vistula. In the middle of the interrogation they lost interest in him; three corporals came into the room and some others arrived and they started to play cards and left Dziobak Przywolski alone till the telephone was mended or Reutenberg came and decided or something.

But he did not leave his captors alone.

Those Germans turned out to be coarse men.

In vain did he try to discern in them even a spark of dark demonic fire : hour after hour they played cards, swore, shot with their submachine guns at a bottle on the gutter of the roof, fried pork in pork fat all night long.

This prisoner, for his part, never stopped talking to all of them. He tried to entertain them and to win their sympathy; he tried to make them laugh, to play his mouth organ for them, even to start an argument. By means of conflicting ideas tending to circularity he attempted to establish some kind of fundamental agreement wih his jailors. After all, both he and they were part of the same perpetual structure, and without either side the structure could never materialize.

14

They were delighted. The spate of high-flown, unintelligible words revived in some of them childhood memories which were vague but strangely sweet. First they gave him beer mixed with salt to drink. This amused them and gave rise to fresh witticisms. They had the idea of dusting him with sneezing powder so as to make him sneeze more and more until he could not stop. Then, slobbering and slurping as they gorged themselves on pork fried in pork fat, they threw crusts of bread at him and feigned innocence. There was great merriment.

There was a babyface among them, pure, pink, and pathetic, who coaxed and implored the guest to turn water into wine, wine into fire, fire into water. And another, a gloomy corporal, a diligent, dedicated schoolboy in a uniform too big for him, looking like Young Werther, stretched out on the filthy floor and pleaded with the sneezing stranger to stop leading them into temptation, for it was too great for them, they were but weak, base matter. There were also numerous drooling drunkards, running with brotherly tears, who tended Dziobak Przywolski continuously, giving him to drink, picking out his lice, and rolling him on to his back and over on to his stomach again. The air was thick with coarse tobacco, frying fat, and stale wine. Till early morning peals of laughter re-echoed, and tears too flowed freely.

The prisoner, however, did not relax his grip on ideas all night long. He addressed them all with devotion and didactic enthusiasm, in excellent, elevated German, speaking at length with both wit and warmth, sneezing frantically, making abundant use of paradox, introducing astounding hypothetical possibilities, arresting syntheses, mathematical speculations, dialectics and more savage sneezes, he conclusively proved that he was of a virgin truly born, they might test him with axe or gun, he was dead and risen again, and sent to bring salvation, vomit and beer were baptism and prayer, atishoo

15

amen, and he wiped their spittle from his face as he groped with words for a synthesis and in desperation even performed a few small miracles, but all in vain.

In short, he with his Germanic thought, with signs and wonders, and they for their part with pork fat.

And yet beneath their uniforms these Germans were nothing but brutish peasants, lumps of clay of Silesia or Lower Saxony, endlessly guzzling beer and staring vacantly into space : cloudy glassy bear's eyes.

Even the lame major, a stuffed Viking with fake gold hair, was an elderly man convulsed with hiccups, who was carried away all that night with high-pitched weeping.

And the guard post itself, formerly a convent or a village seminary, was filthy enough to arouse disgust in a soul which appreciated Culture.

So it happened that Pomeranz suddenly grew tired of his captors.

With an inner shrug he completely abandoned the intellectual confrontation, the synthesis, and in his heart he took his final leave of the nauseating Germans.

Toward morning he began to belch and paw the ground. *Far away in the Promised Land, All our hopes will be fulfilled.* The mouth organ discharged a few sad notes and the man, dreamy and forlorn, rose into the air. Up through the chimney he floated and away into the forest : metaphysical wrong cannot be perceived, while perceptible wrong emits a powerful stench of pork fat.

5

Stefa took Professor Zaicek into her home.

Flaxen-haired Martha, his servant, had abandonèd the scholar's house when the Germans had entered the town. And the Professor, who was adept at discovering hidden links between St Augustine and Friedrich Nietzsche, had never managed to learn to tie his own tie.

He was a lonely, helpless old man. When he bent over the grate to light the fire he covered himself with coal dust, and when he put more coal on he singed the ends of his beard. The smoke blinded him and filled his eyes with tears which buried themselves in his bushy white beard. Despite everything his close friends told him, the Professor continued to maintain the belief that Martha had left him and his house for a man, and that she would be sure to return when her love cooled down. Was that not just what had happened with Martha's cat—she too had disappeared and come back when her time was past. Even his postal links with scattered friends all over Europe progressively deteriorated. Worst of all, the Goethe Society had ceased to function, and the Goetheans themselves seemed to have vanished into thin air.

Perhaps they had all fled to the cellars, to the forests, and only he was forgotten?

There, in their dark hideout, by candlelight, all the Goetheans would be meeting every night and holding whispered conferences. They would draw up a sensational document which would instantly bring the world back to its senses. Germany herself would open her eyes and be smitten with shame. And meanwhile Stefa came; the drunken gardener, Run-Jesus, piled several suitcases, bags, files of documents, photographs and woollen underwear on a small handcart, and that night the Professor was taken into Stefa's house. Times were not easy.

And so toward sunset, as evening came down, while Martha Pinch-me-not abandoned herself to the arms of clerks or moustached policemen, while the Goetheans in their candlelit cellar fitted word to word with supreme care, the Professor would stand alone at the window for half an hour or more, and contemplate the fading of day. He could see the damp grey wind howling across the town of M——, bursting out over wide wintry expanses, stirring the fir forests, screeching at cottage windows. Far away in the distance he could see huts and towers, and beyond them the lights of Warsaw gradually dying away, the swell of the turbid Baltic, night stooping over Berlin, steep ravines darkening in alpine valleys, he could sense the mighty rivers flowing through the dark, Volga, Rhine, darkness on the peaks of the Pyrenees and Apennines, darkness on the northern steppes and the mountains of the Balkans, and over all, bitter and piercing, the howling of steppe wolves at solitary towers. Then Stefa would gently touch his shoulder. Professor Zaicek would start, bow deeply to his watch, peering to make it out, and announce :

'It is dark outside.'

Stefa would draw the heavy curtains, put on the lights, lead the scholar to an armchair, and offer them both a drink. The Karl Marx features, touched by wisdom and agony, would brighten slowly, painfully, as though by a powerful effort of the will, until they finally suggested the hint of a shy smile. Stefa would say :

'A pleasant evening.'

And the Professor, dreamily, gently, somewhat distantly, would hasten to respond :

'A pleasant evening, Stefa, yes indeed.'

How Stefa loved the flavour of those first mornings.

She would bring him a hot cup of coffee in bed, and Professor Zaicek, however early she came, would always be waiting for her, his blue eyes wide open, and would remark in carefully chosen words on the beauty of the morning and the purity and purifying power of the birdsong coming from the garden. She would help him out of bed, brush and comb his thick beard, tie his tie, straighten his cuffs and pat a little Eau de Cologne into his prophetic mane. Then she would take his arm and lead to the breakfast table a magnificent, well-groomed old man, thoroughly prepared to face a new day.

At bedtime she would sit by his bedside, a cool intellectual beauty, and softly sing him, in a peasant-girl accent, some of the folk songs which flaxen-haired Martha used to sing him : only these songs could lull him into the arms of innocent slumber. Barefoot and erect in her nightgown she would slip into his bedroom around midnight to see that his night light had not gone out. His regular childlike breathing instilled a sense of peace in Stefa.

Days and weeks passed, and from time to time at unforeseen moments there may suddenly have been a slight touch : her hand may have brushed against his, a melody touching a ruin.

All day long the old man sat silently in front of the fire, lost in thought. At his feet the two cats, Chopin and Schopenhauer, lay curled up together sleeping. Martha would soon come back. The winter would pass. In Jaroslaw Avenue the chestnut trees would blossom, log-laden rafts would drift once again down the river, and anglers would sit motionless on the bank. Meanwhile the wind howled outside, because it was winter and this was a wintry place.

Stefa would say :

'It is as if time were standing still, the days go by so slowly.'

Professor Zaicek:

'And even though the room is so warm, my feet are frozen.'

Stefa:

'How about some brandy. Or some tea. '

Zaicek:

'Yes indeed, Stefa, that ink you bought yesterday was watered. And in the middle of the night there was a tinkling sound. Who is mending glass in the street at night?'

Sometimes toward evening the Professor would summon up hidden reserves of strength; he would rise from his chair and pace to and fro with porcelain footsteps on the rug, a little woollen skullcap secured to his mane with a hairpin, dictating a thought or two to Stefa. Afterward Stefa was requested to play the piano, and he, huddled and racked with agony, looking like a wizened embryo curled up in a jar, would suddenly challenge Nietzsche's view of the birth of tragedy from the spirit of music. His words were joined together with a hushed pathos, and when he stopped talking and turned his back on the room to stare out of the darkening window, Stefa felt that the air was charged. All that winter he was carving out in his mind the materials for a future work on the painful relationships between people. All the various relationships: Man and woman. Father and son. Brothers. Casual tennis partners. Master and slave. Teacher and pupil. Persecutor and victim. Lover and beloved. Pair of strangers.

As Professor Zaicek spoke, Stefa was sometimes certain that a special smell emanated together with his words and filled the room, a tough brown smell, like the smell of dying chestnut leaves in autumn.

Darkness came, feeling its way with long fingers of twilight, spreading like black death over all Europe, over streams and birch trees, over shuttered cities and desolate tundras, over Poland and its forests, and into the room, creeping under the armchairs, round the cats, the shelves, the ornaments, the pink Matisse girl, the African warrior threatening her, the gleam in the eye of the stuffed bear, darkness in Professor Zaicek's low sad voice, affirming in unambiguous syntax the circularity of all laws, unravelling the tangled ties between death and madness, love and mercy. Mystical reasoning. Take this very evening, he would say, both here and everywhere.

And night like a heavy cloak settled on the town of M——, enfolding the wounded belfry of St Stephen's Church, subduing the dockyards and charging them with restless massivity, pressing heavily on the shattered fountain in Magdalen Lane, clasping into its desperate embrace Jaroslaw Avenue, the Concert Hall, the wooden shacks in the outskirts, the guards in their menacing greatcoats, the river, blackening the snow-covered fields, weaving a forest spell over the town, and turning the town to forest.

6

Furthermore.

Stefa was so surprised she could scarcely believe her eyes: an antique Gothic clock without hands adorned the corner of the drawing room, and now suddenly Professor Zaicek with his own brittle fingers had succeeded in making it utter a few dim chimes from its depths.

Just like Pomeranz, then, who had fled to the forests, Professor Zaicek, too, was the son of a watchmaker. Who of them isn't, Stefa asked herself. There was once a little song current in some of the villages, which bore popular testimony to the connection between Jews and watches:

> *Good morning, fine morning, my dear Mr Jew,*
> *Let me propose a small deal to you:*
> *You have a watch, I have a hatchet—*
> *Throw me your watch and see if I catch it.*

The Professor suddenly recalled the song, but he supposed that Stefa neither knew it nor wanted to; so he restrained himself and merely hummed the tune into his beard, and in his usual fashion, as if it involved an extraordinary physical effort, he summoned up the ghost of a smile. While outside in the dark in the snow a heavily wrapped German patrol went by.

Conditions deteriorated week by week and almost day by day. Occasionally Stefa fought back a sob. A loaf of rye bread cost four zlotys. The drunken gardener Run-Jesus chopped down the apple trees in the garden to keep the fire burning for a few days longer. And he exacted the price of his silence with ever more menacing cheerfulness. At dawn the sky glowed red from distant fires around the town. An elderly humanist complained that a German soldier had called him a name in one of the main streets of the town in broad daylight. A hundred and six shaven-headed orphans were taken from the orphanage and transported in a cattle truck to a holiday camp by the Black Sea, some said to Madagascar. The town was alive with wild speculations, rumours, black-marketeering, and primitive superstitions.

The military governor of the town, General Baron von Topf, instructed his staff to examine the town register carefully and draw up a complete and detailed list of individuals actively involved in music. On the basis of this list the General Baron formed a private orchestra of burghers, in addition to the circle of historians which was summoned to meet for brief discussions in the governor's office at extraordinarily early hours of the morning.

So it was that every Sunday an eager band performed

in the square in front of St Stephen's Church, and a German loudspeaker cheerfully invited the audience to take the floor. He also ordered the Mother Superior Felicitas to be stigmatized—in the old meaning of the word—at the ruins of the belfry. He wished to conduct an experiment : it had occurred to him to settle once and for all a thousand-year-old controversy, whether or not there was any truth in the common belief that the Virgin had bestowed a particular grace on the Polish cross. And if she had, whether the state of grace still obtained. And because a method cannot be based on a single case, von Topf continued to experiment in various different ways. He was passionately devoted to the twilight zone between theology and metaphysics. According to a rumour, he was learning, or trying to learn, Hebrew at night. Moreover, he had been attracted by nuns since his early youth.

Professor Zaicek said to Stefa :

'It is my duty to speak to him. The situation must be clarified. You must invite him here one day, Stefa my dear, for a talk, for tea, so that we can demand an explanation.'

Stefa said :

'That would be a terrible risk. Even your papers are not your own.'

The old man reflected, and admitted the fact. For a while he absently stroked one of the Siamese cats, then he leaned back and continued gently stroking the arm of his chair. How he wanted not to sound melodramatic, yet to use words that Stefa would never be able to forget, even in her dreams. Finally he spoke :

'But Stefa. Surely. We didn't run away to the forest, did we? And why did we both refuse to run away? Surely, dearest Stefa, it was because the word danger has no external validity. We have taught time and again, and recently we have even committed it to print, that the real danger is always from within. And have we the right, my wonderful Stefa, to turn our backs on our own teaching? Surely there are moments in the life of an individual or of a people when silence is an abhorrent misuse of speech. No, Stefa, no, my dear, no, here we are and here we stand and we cannot be otherwise. In the face of evil, we must stand up and say: evil! Now it's time for tea.'

Primly but eagerly, almost gaily, Stefa clapped her hands, only the corners of her mouth betraying a new determination.

'Yes, teatime, my dear Professor; I am sure you have been waiting for your tea. Won't you take your place at the head of the table; here comes your napkin, and your teaspoon, and here's the samovar.'

She tied the napkin round his neck to protect his brown jacket, put his teaspoon in his hand, deftly removed a silver hair from his shoulder, poured two cups of tea, and nodded to Professor Zaicek to give the sign.

The sage asked in vain for butter: times were not easy. So he gave the sign for them to start, took a hesitant sip, and said:

'Kindly put on the light. And in the study too. After tea I want to dictate a letter to Martin Heidegger. His position is a great mystery to me. I deliberately refrain from saying a disappointment. A Socratic letter. That is to say, I shall put a few questions to him. Questions and nothing more. Yes, Stefa, of course I shall lower my voice as you request, but I shall not stop talking. As for compromises, my dear, you and I could both get up tomorrow morning and leave for America or Palestine as if to say that evil disgusts us but is none of our business. But that is not what we have taught, that is not what we have written, that is not what we have determined. It is madness to think of evil as the private affair of the evil man, just as hunger is not the private affair of the starving man or disease that of the invalid, nor is death the problem of the dead, but of the living, and that means us, my one and only Stefa. The thermometer fell again today, and apparently therefore it is getting colder. You ought to devote a moment's thought to Martin Luther. Luther was vulgar and ignorant, and yet he offers us a surprisingly clever way out of the moral dilemma. But should we, my Stefa, casually take this cheap way out? No, Stefa, no, my dear, we shall hold fast to our course even in the midst of this great darkness. There's that glass tinkling again in the street – in the garden – as if all of a sudden there are pieces of glass hanging from the branches of the trees and the wind makes them tinkle. What is it, Stefa, what does the tinkling signify, if indeed it signifies anything at all?'

Stefa said:

'I can't hear any tinkling. The windows are closed and shuttered. There's nothing there.'

The Karl Marx face, furrowed by wisdom and agony, seemed to brighten and darken and brighten again in the flickering light, and the warm voice spread through the room as if seeking the darkness beyond the shuttered windows. How can he, thought Stefa, how can he ask me to put on all the lights. Now. These are almost the last days. There is no more time.

In that instant a tortured, emaciated form floated soundlessly into the room, grinning from ear to ear, the drunken gardener who was nicknamed Run-Jesus. He bowed twice, first to his master and mistress and then to the wall, perhaps to the stuffed bear's head. He laid some damp logs in the grate, grinned another depraved grin, displaying his rotting teeth, and exacted his wages and the price of his silence from Stefa. Suddenly he began to plead, with short sharp sobs and hoarse coughs, sounds which resembled the barking of a fox:

'Multiplying beyond all bounds, they are. No one to keep an eye on them, that's what. Like bedbugs they're spreading. Millions of them. Laughing they are, too, the dogs' blood. What's so funny here, eh? Won't be long before we'll all have to sleep standing up, won't even have room to lie down at night. There's a thousand of 'em born every minute. And as soon as they're born they start breeding. Into their own mothers' wombs, the sons of bitches. And how they breed. Like a plague. Holy Mary forgive me for what I'm saying. Is there enough water for us and for them, eh? No, there's not. Dogs' blood, there's not. Look at me, now, I'm a sick man, sick through and through, my poor legs, and then there's the coughing, and what's more I'm a sinner, but don't I deserve a drop of water same as anyone else? Millions of 'em. More and more born every minute, some says a thousand, some says more, church mice can't hold a light to 'em. And what's the upshot? Millions of them'll die of thirst. Not enough water. Not enough room to stand up in, even. Not enough air to breathe. And on Tuesday I brought you eggs and potatoes, and if God Almighty wills it, there'll be feathers, too. Not to mention the flour. And suppose the river dries up, what'll they drink then, eh? And that lot'll breathe up all the air too, and we'll all suffocate, grrr, like leprous dogs. It's cold tonight, good Sir and Madam, it's very cold, very very cold. Jesus guard me from this cold. Me, I'm a sick man, a coughing man, and I'll tell you a secret, I'm dogs' blood too. But Jesus won't laugh at me. It's stupid for us to laugh, good Sir and Madam, stupid, sinful, indecent, nothing to laugh at here while that lot, curse 'em, breed and breed without a moment's pause. Christ's blessing on you both.'

Furiously poised on the sideboard stood a carved African warrior covered in war paint. Day and night the savage threatened the terrified girl in the Matisse painting with his huge, grotesque manhood. And from above, the bear's head, amazingly silent, looked down.

The glass eyes reflected the candlelight and shot back flashing sparks.

7

Once again the tranquillity of dark forests. The night wind's caress. The silent frost. The squelching mud. Flight without escape. If you strike with all your might, the axe will break.

Beneath the crust of ice lurk different forces, far from the nature of ice and far from peace and rest. Powerful forces which cannot be exorcized by formulae or incantations. Even music gradually abandons you night by night and flows into the night and with the powers of night it grinds its teeth at you.

Deep in the evil Polish forest deep in the heart of the darkness deep in the womb of the soggy undergrowth can be seen shadows of giant creepers clasping and choking the dead tree trunks with silent fury as though squeezing the last drops from a desperate loving embrace.

And the wide wastes resound with the frantic howling of wolves.

Pomeranz had suddenly had enough.

He was tired of wandering, tired of peasants, of Germans, of the soughing fir trees, of fleeing like a sick animal.

And the snow and the fire and the wind.

So he played his mouth organ at them with all his might and main, until the Russians heard and burst across all the rivers in their way, San, Bug, Wisla.

And the war ended.

Blood poisoning. Pneumonia. Exhaustion.

Large peasants with broad sashes and clay pipes, suspicious men with bushy whiskers, took Pomeranz to a
tumbledown hospital in northern Hungary. It was in a
long narrow valley, a swampy region fed by the Car-
pathian streams. Here they raised lean pigs and strange
vegetables, and an alarming number of the children
were deformed from birth.

The barracks of the ducal regiment were now a revolutionary hospital, or it may originally have been stables.
The walls were daubed with crooked Magyar crosses.
At the top of each cross someone had pinned brightly
coloured pictures of the fathers of the Russian Revolution. The portraits had been hurriedly or clumsily torn
from some propaganda pamphlet, and their outlines
were irregular.

Pomeranz was laid on two sacks of straw. His groin
and armpits were sprayed with DDT and he was given
antisyphilis tablets from the stocks left behind by the
Germans. No other medicines were available as yet.

There was a Ruthenian doctor, as tiny as a grass-
hopper and wrecked by nicotine. He believed with
perfect faith that Dziobak Przywolski was indeed the
son of a virgin and that he had risen from the dead. But
then he also ascribed virgin birth to Stalin, to the Polish
Marshal Smigly-Rydz, to several local herdsmen, and,
finally—in a sudden fit of high-pitched fury—to himself
as well.

In sum, the unwashed Ruthenian doctor argued that
every proletarian, provided he was not Pontius Pilate
or Judas Iscariot, must be Jesus. He argued by elimina-

tion: if you are not Jesus, who are you? To support this opinion, and also his claim to be the inventor of aspirin, he produced a parchment scroll written and sealed in a Ukrainian dialect, and he insisted that this same dialect had been used by the writer Gogol in his early works.

All the doctor's ideas were enthusiastically seconded by a one-armed organist, a local man, who was indisputably related to the Bach family; he had once made his living by eating live flies in a cabaret in Budapest, and now he was in the habit of kicking at every door and shouting, Serve them right, serve them right, they've got their just deserts, load of skunks, everything that's hit them on land and sea and air is only a foretaste of the punishment that's waiting for them in Heaven, in the Angelic Realm, even outside the Solar System, if you'll all just keep quiet for a moment you'll hear for yourselves the sound of the knives being sharpened.

Pomeranz lay very quiet. He was regaining his strength. The place gave him perfect rest and healing. His mouth organ lay untouched.

One night, by the light of a crazed Hungarian candle, the Ruthenian entered, neighing wildly, bringing the virgin Mary herself to the invalid's bed. She smelled of milk and rye and goat dung, and she was lacking most of her teeth. Pomeranz opened his eyes wide, tore her sackcloth off her, inhaled her smell, Jewish loneliness suddenly flooded him so that his soul wanted to burst out howling. But his watchmaker's fingers retained their precision and expertise. They brought the virgin Mary to shrill giggles, pleading whimpers, desperate sighs, she began to revel with her legs with her teeth with her nails. The doctor and his friend the organist stood beside the ragged palliasse and shielded the cavorting flame from the wind with their hands as a wild draft swept through the cellar and they sang Ave Maria in harmony like an angelic choir until the vision was fulfilled and the holy virgin was led out of the stable laughing cursing dripping blood sweat and tears.

Pomeranz recovered, too. He got up and continued on his way, to *the Land where Spring reigns eternal.*

9

Where is that land, that Promised Land, Joy of the World, our journey's end?

Pomeranz now carried several new sets of documents:
Bulgarian.
Polish.
Red Cross.
Jewish Agency.
Red Partisan Brotherhood.

And he sometimes had whole packages of Rumanian cigarettes. A Russian greatcoat. Superbly German fur-lined boots. And, what was more, a pair of woollen gloves from the Joint Distribution Committee. It was a slow, lunatic journey, through the length and breadth of the Balkans. As if his soul's inner flow had been beset by a sudden stammer, a need to linger, to prepare, to settle something once and for all. He tried in Vienna. He tried in South Tyrol. And once, in a Zionist refugee hostel named after Max Nordau, Pomeranz happened to hear the gospel from his Promised Land. David Ben-Gurion, on his way to London, stayed overnight and addressed the survivors, passionately and with the fervour of inner conviction, *a fire blazing in our breasts, human chaff will once again become a nation, we shall rebuild the Temple, set the land aflame with a blaze of green.*

Pomeranz was almost tempted to take out his mouth organ and play an accompaniment.

Only, the next morning persistent rumours spread among the refugees that it had not been Ben-Gurion at all, but someone else, an impersonator, a double, a dummy sent to draw the assassins' fire.

So the dreamy son of a watchmaker began frantically buying and selling bales of cloth. For the time being. In private he belched and belched. The mouth organ lay untouched. Was there still a mouth organ, or was that too perhaps a double, a deliberate imposture?

Now he only worked wonders when no one was looking. And he restricted himself to minor, trivial actions, like lighting a cigarette with a fountain pen, or soothing an aching tooth. He would not have hesitated to steal chickens left and right, if there had been any chickens to steal.

And sold them for lire. And changed them into drachmas. Converted to dollars. For the time being.

In Piraeus he was involved for some days and weeks with Polish deserters who were smuggling parts for sewing machines from port to port, westward toward Marseille. His job was to remove the rust, to stamp them with false names, to paint them convincing colours. The deserters, who were mostly old sailors, called Pomeranz Mieczyslaw the First, because they ecstatically believed that the Princess Magda Izawolska had conceived an illegitimate child by the late Pope, and that he was her son.

Indeed, one night they anointed him with sewing-machine oil King of the New Poland. The tavern walls shook all night long with the sounds of cheering and singing. There was a rumour that the Americans were on the point of setting up a new kingdom of Poland in the Aegean Islands under the protection of the Ninth Airborne Division. Until circumstances changed. And when the right time came, they would join Greece to the Baltic by a gigantic canal.

The deserters were preparing for the dawn of the new Poland, purifying their souls, enthusiastically anticipating the great moment, dedicatedly stealing whatever they might need on the day, clothing, food, wine, rifles and pistols, and especially flags and bugles. Pomeranz, for his part, ran a printing press and produced quantities of Swiss promissory notes.

He said to himself:

Wine, sardines, women, greatcoat, cigarettes, you've got everything for nothing. They don't demand anything from you in return. And if some stars suddenly wake up and start singing in the distance before dawn, why, all you have to do is stand alone on the quayside in Piraeus till daybreak, concentrate hard, and listen in perfect silence. You don't need to give any answer. This is Greece. The New Kingdom of Poland. Just say good night to the American sentry. Accept a cigarette. Przywolski the Last or Mieczyslaw the First, stand and smoke with your collar turned up. And because the sea is close at hand, proffer the glowing stub to the black water.

10

Stefa and the Professor jointly sent a lengthy and anguished letter of complaint to Professor Heidegger. Among other things they propounded a model for a hypothetical synthesis between suffering and the will: a kind of reciprocity, a new definition of the subjective-objective relationship in a sphere laden with will and suffering.

This letter, owing to the circumstances, went astray and failed to reach the philosopher.

Conditions worsened considerably. Snow, torture, and suppressed rage besieged the town of M——.

The night wind hounded everything with its venomous fangs. Railways trucks left laden at night and next morning came back empty. Slowacski, Copernicus, and

Pilsudski were torn from the street names. Even the chestnut trees were torn up to feed fires. Jews were taken from the town to learn productive labour to train them for their Palestine. Ukrainian peasants brought from far away toiled night and day in the workshops, machine-gun nests were set up on hills and rooftops, barbed-wire fences divided Jaroslaw Avenue, even the park benches were torn up and carted off to the foundry. Through the patchy fog thin tall tongues of flame could be seen rising from distant villages. The town grew ugly and flat.

Worst of all, the military governor, General Baron von Topf, found himself somewhat indisposed. On account of the damp climate, on account of the heavy burden of responsibility, on account of the weight of official obligations, on account of the narrowing of cultural horizons, a repulsive growth developed.

Frantic doctors came and went by day and by night. There was a consultation. A written opinion was even solicited from Professor Sauerbruch in Berlin. Meanwhile the offending growth thickened and spread : it sprouted from one of the lower vertebrae, it caused endless unpleasantness and embarrassment, and demanded humiliating subterfuges, it filled out the trousers, it hung obstinately down and could only with great difficulty be persuaded to conceal itself inside the knee-boot, it was warm and wilful and brown, it was a frightening, indecent appendage, a hairy, outrageous postfix, which wriggled vigorously at the General Baron's command and for the most part even against his explicit orders, a mischievous extrusion, at one and the same time dependent and independent, flouting the rules of good taste and military discipline alike, and breaking free from the well-pressed trousers, a source of shame and anger.

In short, a tail.

So it was that the Baron von Topf gradually began to display less warmth toward the town's intelligentsia.

He who had set up the historical circle and the orchestra and arranged theosophical debates. There were incidents which offended against good taste by any standards. For example :

A dinner party was arranged in the old castle, behind the grim stone walls raised to the glory of the kings of Poland. All the leading members of the intelligentsia were invited by the governor. Not one of them saw fit to decline the invitation and thus detract from their collective good manners. A special pass entitled the intelligentsia to be abroad that night during the hours of curfew. The French chef of the Huntsman's Inn was summoned to work miracles. The guests were conveyed in evening dress to the forbidden side of the bridge and at the entrance to Kazimierz Hall the sentries saluted. There were four identical vases on each table, and each vase held five symmetrically arranged chrysanthemums. The staff officers appeared, spotlessly turned out; the town orchestra was ready and waiting. The master of ceremonies entered, stood to attention and announced the adjutant, who entered, stood to attention and announced the military governor, General Baron von Topf, who limped hurriedly to the head of the table, sat down, and motioned the company to be at their ease. The governor had a sensational piece of news to announce : just before the dinner, literally at the last moment, it had been discovered that the president of the Goethe Society, the eminent philosopher Professor Zaicek, was residing in the town in circumstances of extreme obscurity, turning his back on his many admirers of both nationalities; and they were to be highly honoured, the governor's own official car had already been sent to fetch the great man, and here he was. The Baron clicked his heels, bowed to the thinker and kissed his companion's hand, and exchanged pleasantries as he escorted them both to their places. Music.

It may be added that as an exotic touch a real Russian bear captured in the region of Smolensk had also been

34

urgently summoned to be present. Among the topics discussed over dinner was the problem of causality, and the guests were not spared some surprising developments. In the course of the discussion, which was conducted in elaborate German, Professor Zaicek, along with the other guests, was served with hock and caviar, and the guest from Russia was served with the Professor. At once the bear was tried by court-martial, presided over by General Baron von Topf with a Polish defence counsel and a German staff officer prosecuting. The accused himself behaved in a thoroughly shaggy and silent manner throughout the trial, displaying a grim Russian stoicism and an almost morbid attitude in every gesture. While the case was being heard he seemed drowsy, somewhat gloomy, heavy, and distinctly Slavic. With sharp knives he was stripped of his Bolshevik pelt and his meat was served up garnished with almonds and crumbled egg yolk. And the guests were given a free choice between red and white wine.

Later on the armed guards, and the adjutant's instructions, put out all the lights, and the party continued in darkness till daylight. The Polish intelligentsia, in their habitual way, were consumed with self-pity, tragic emotion, and theatrical grandeur. Indeed, outside, below the castle windows, several trucks were drawn up waiting for the guests to leave. Stefa, for her part, was ordered to play the piano. In obedience to a polite command she played till the night was done, Chopin, Schubert, fantasies and variations, agitation submission and rebellion, a marriage of souls in melancholy splendour between Poles and Germans, pork cooked in pork fat.

In sum, that night changed something in Stefa. A certain hardening. A certain closeness to the dreamy son of a watchmaker. If she only knew if and where.

Toward dawn a stranger entered and took Stefa by the arm. He bowed twice, assumed a well-modulated waiter's smile, politely escorted Stefa down into the underground levels of the ancient castle, through mossy cellars, twisting caverns deep below the walls, winding staircases, a rock-hewn labyrinth, among rust-eaten shields and bleached human bones, the stinking depths of Poland, onward, eastward, into the rising sun we march, a new dawn will break over the forests, the landscape will brighten again, golden wheatfields stretching into the distance, onward, always eastward.

The stranger was amazingly thin, deadly-looking, and extremely tall. He protected Stefa all along the way and saw her safely, and just in time, behind the Russian lines.

Large, laughing peasant women greeted her with their languorous songs, everywhere accompanied by the sweet sadness of the balalaika.

And the war ended.

II

Promised Land:

There to live in liberty, there to flourish, pure and free, there our hopes shall be fulfilled—thought through action may be stilled.

Death to the nightmares, *look the light in the eye,* make a new start in the blue brightness of summer. Settle. Down. In Sharon, rose of Sharon blooming, in the valley, lily of the valley, and on the mountains, the feet of the messenger. And the thin, mischievous moustache will come off once and for all. Start a new life. Reconciled, back to the land, youth regained, healing for body and soul, rest for the weary, balm for the wounded, let there be light.

In 1949, after several painful experiences, Pomeranz

36

was finally forced to the realization that the only safe refuge for a Jew was in his own state in his own ancestral land, and so the wandering Jew arrived at last in Israel. He had some savings, in various Balkan currencies and in dollars, and he had also acquired on his travels a certain business sense. But he did not set his sights high. He wanted to live in the country, to work on the land, in peace. To find his own level. He determined to earn his living somehow, somewhere, while he prepared his body and his soul for working on the land, perhaps in a kibbutz. For the time being he was given a one-room apartment in Tiberias, overlooking the Sea of Galilee, in an Arab house whose occupants had fled.

He found a small secure shop in a narrow side street which seemed to suit his purpose. He rented it, cleaned it out, decorated it, he lavished his savings on a counter and shelves, a fan, a chair, a picture, he arranged the shop, rearranged it, his whole body trembling with the effort and the passion.

When the preparations were complete he excitedly printed on a large card a two-word Hebrew poem :

POMERANZ
WATCHMAKER

Pomeranz was forty-three years old when he wrote these words. For an instant he suddenly experienced a belated love. Something inside him was swept away, dissolved, released.

Next he settled on a routine. The bars on the outside of his window curved in rusty arabesques. He painted them. He revived the geraniums in the window boxes. The low ceiling, arching gently above his head, seemed to be trying to testify to Emanuel Zaicek's theory of universal circularity.

No longer young, starting new daily habits in a new

37

place, in an alien climate, surrounded by unfamiliar objects. A need for great caution in small things, buying a brush, plugging in the tall thin kettle, crossing the road, the strange salesmen and policemen, the neighbours' dogs and children, duplicated circulars in Hebrew script.

Opposite his shop there was a garage for automobile repairs. A rickety shed. There was a young man working there, almost a boy, with sunburned skin and a moustache. Pomeranz stared at him from his shop because this handsome, self-confident youth was in the habit of talking to himself. When there was no one else about in the garage, generally during the hottest hours of the day, Pomeranz could see him through his shop window bending over a heap of junk, kicking, muttering, making a pleading gesture with his hand, then cancelling it with a wave of dismissal, raising his hand to his face as if at the sight of a calamity, drooping his head, shoulders, and arms in despair, once more muttering, then suddenly clapping his hand to his mouth and disappearing hurriedly into the shed. The air was full of the smell of dust steeped with grease and gasoline, of metal being soldered in sweltering heat, the painful groan of an engine refusing to start.

The work of mending watches and clocks brought about a cool feeling of enjoyment, a gradual rallying of the forces of order. It was an experience resembling convalescence, an almost mathematical delight, something approaching music.

He would focus a narrow beam of light on his work, fix a magnifying glass in his left eye socket, pick up a fine pair of tweezers. His hands had learned to be calm and controlled. Time that was out of joint he set right, and restored a steady movement. Sometimes he took the pleasure he got from the work into account when fixing the price of a repair.

After work he went home, put on a clean shirt, and

served himself bread, yoghurt, fresh dates, and coffee. He sat back in the rocking chair he had bought, and gazed out the window for an hour or two at the swaying curves of the palm trees, at the distant mountains and at their reflection in the water of the lake. Slowly, with great caution, he debated with the blazing light, and with the alien, disturbing landscape. Negotiating, considering terms, bargaining formulae, examining alternative suggestions, perpetually on his guard against baits and snares. It was a fascinating, if tiring, procedure. Gradually there was a healing, because Europe was far away, and the refuge seemed, so far as any refuge could be, safe and secure.

Journey's end, Pomeranz said to himself.

Time passed, and Pomeranz, still squinting, still dreamy, began to resume his old researches, which he had neglected for more than ten years now, somewhere in the twilight zone between pure mathematics and theoretical physics. The way back was difficult and exhausting, because here, overlooking the Sea of Galilee, the very figures seemed to play a different tune. Mathematical arabesques.

In spring, in autumn, and even on beautiful winter days, Pomeranz was in the habit of taking a short walk as the day ended. Gentle and pensive as a westerly breeze, as a distant caress, he passed through the streets of Tiberias, testing with the tip of his cane the solidity of a park bench, of the paving stones, tapping the trunk of a palm tree and standing motionless for a moment, with his eyes closed and his senses strained. Perhaps he would hear an answer.

Was it not conceivable that it would happen here, a hint, a sound, a sign?

Sometimes his wanderings led him to the shore of the darkening lake, near a wooden jetty or a little fishing harbour. Here he would stand for a long while, as the shadows enfolded him, looking like a secret agent in a preliminary reconnaissance.

He would turn to go, nodding his head, as if caught up in a complicated inner debate.

On his way back up the hill he would linger, trying to count the birds shrilling in the trees, solemnly contemplating the view of the darkening mountains on the other side of the lake, committing as many details as possible to memory. Then he would head for home.

Tiberias seemed to him an insubstantial town, built on shallow foundations, perhaps hesitating between two contrasting rhythms. Tall palm trees reaching longingly skyward; low arches bowing and prostrating themselves. But surely the haughtiness of the palms and the submissiveness of the arches were simply two different expressions of the same underlying idea.

Here and there the authorities had set up green-painted benches, surrounded by a few pathetic plants and a display of written prohibitions. Here and there somebody had begun to put up a monumental building, but had had second thoughts when he reached the second storey, realized what he had not seen at the outset, and changed his mind. Flimsy housing developments spread up the hillside month by month. Little square matchboxes, uniformly whitewashed, like a drawing by an unimaginative child. Neat row upon neat row, apartment houses, submitting to the harsh rule of the white summer light and obediently offering their whiteness in return. Pomeranz had no difficulty in understanding this sudden Jewish passion for neatness. For whitewash. For clean-cut lines. For simplicity and uncompromising brightness. For building here and just so and quickly, without any concession to the rolling hills and gently curving domes. Tense as a clenched fist. And if the earth curves and arches beneath us, if hills softly ripple beneath the modern streets, then surely this undulation will merely serve to excite still further the *fire blazing in our breasts,* and *set the land aflame with a blaze of green.*

40

The lake, for its part, sometimes roused feelings of nostalgia, and at times he could sense a passing breeze of silent, elusive mockery.

Then, night by night, the sly conspiracy of the stars against a crescent moon. The night wind had a message to deliver, and Pomeranz concentrated and strained his senses.

There were, naturally, superficial relations with four or five people. The grocer, who at six o'clock would listen to two different news broadcasts simultaneously on two radio sets, in French and Arabic, who was surrounded by piles of newspapers and magazines, and was daily expecting a major disaster. Pomeranz would exchange a few sentences with him, bloodcurdling political speculations, apocalyptic forecasts, international conspiracies and manœuvres. Then there were the meter readers, the neighbours, their dogs, their children, regular and occasional customers. They all crossed his path without impinging on him, because he did not want to encroach or to make friends, but only to sit quietly and calculate, sit and silently listen.

The summer in Tiberias was long and white-hot. For nine or ten months everything roasted in an opaque white glare, and a fine dust filled the air; in the morning crowds of birds ran amok, and at midday even a handrail would scorch the hand that touched it. All summer long, dark men swarmed the streets, exuding a warm, brown peaceful smell like freshly baked bread. To Pomeranz their presence was amazing, not Jewish, but not Gentile either; it called for cautious observation and a new exertion of the senses. Slowly. Without taking risks.

He would suddenly remember snow. From here it seemed to him an absurd, lunatic image, perhaps a painted scene in an old-fashioned opera. The snow-capped peak of Mount Hermon which could sometimes

41

be seen from Tiberias reminded him of the cheap gaudy oil paintings which peasants who had made good hung in their new houses, above the pianos on which their daughters were forced to practise to the point of despair.

Tiberias smelled of baking fish in the afternoon, and of rotting fish at night. And at almost every hour of the night and day there blew from the lake a slight, stubborn smell of putrefaction. Peanuts, fizzy lemonade, lottery tickets, chocolate-ices, Egged buses, evening papers—all constantly clamoured for recognition, at least *de facto*.

In contrast to all this there were hints of an entirely different presence. It was commonly believed and persistently maintained that close at hand, just beyond the boulder-strewn slopes opposite, on the other side of the scorched mountain range, lay the veiled city of Damascus, and Abana and Pharpar, its rivers. Springs and fountains, myrrh and frankincense almost within touching distance.

The need to guard against nostalgia.

Concentrate your attention on the here-and-now: Tiberias, summer, Israel, nineteen-fifty-one, opposite an automobile repair shop, twenty past two in the afternoon, twenty-one minutes past, twenty-two, a cigarette and a bottle of lemonade. And the boy across the street arguing with himself among his junk, and the air full of the smell of dust steeped with grease and gasoline.

Thousands of Jews living in broad daylight in Tiberias, openly, unashamed, with no second line of defence, no bunkers, no split-second disguises, no secret way out, as if it were all over and done with. To the dreamy son of a watchmaker the whole situation was terrible and wonderful. An inconceivable state of affairs, which the heart longed to believe.

Occasionally he tried to sense from a distance, using his thoughts like radar beams, his faraway town of M——. Steeples, bells, and forests. The smell of Stefa's

fur coat. Jaroslaw Avenue. The statue of Copernicus.
The piles of the bridge and the black river. The attempt
was doomed to failure. Those places did not exist and
never had existed, because they could not exist and never
could have.

But this place, this real place, this hot, panting place,
the paraffin cart with its bell, the health clinic, the
traffic policeman, the carpet of peanut shells, ration
cards, queuing for flour, the smell of fish, and these
big brown Jews—could this place possibly exist?

12

The stranger who steered Stefa by the arm and politely
escorted her eastward toward the Russian lines was
suspiciously tall thin and deadly. He was no more than
a black tail-coat, starched shirt-front, and white tie.

The whole devastated continent seemed to yield to
him in total obedience : German guards saluted and
made way, officers offered their services, detectives,
gendarmes, partisan bands provided guides through the
dense forests and shared their food and wine, fisher-
men ferried them on rafts, peasants lavished hospitality,
commissars went out of their way to assist and to please,
onward always eastward, toward peasant women joy-
fully gathering potatoes, toward wide-stretching corn-
fields into the rising sun.

Stefa was handed over to the Revolutionary Bureau
for Polish Affairs in Krasnoyarsk. After a few simple
tests a use was found for her. At first she was set to
work editing various publications in Polish, pamphlets,
an Open Letter to the Reluctant Intellectual, an address
to the workers engaged in rebuilding the ruins of
Warsaw, a letter from the Central Committee to the

writers of the New Poland on their great day.

This was just a modest beginning. It was not what she was born for.

Soon she could be seen with visiting Polish intellectuals at the theatre, in the coffee houses, or boating on the lake, resplendent in evening dress and jet earrings. Stefa could arouse a wild fervour in her guests : in her company they all talked compulsively, some of them seemed fired by grandiose visions and battered her with complex combinations of ideas, others were poetically inspired and painted grandiloquent pictures of a heavenly Warsaw, a new kingdom of Poland in the Aegean Islands, a synthesis of rival salvations, while Stefa ruthlessly egged them on, drawing the very marrow out of their bones, until the Polish intellectuals sank into a delicious weariness. She had to restrain them forcibly from kneeling down and kissing her feet; she escorted them back to their hotels; they always collapsed as if drunk into a chair in the hotel foyer, and she returned home well after midnight.

Next morning she would draw up a report. Single out, categorize, appraise, recommend :

One way or the other.

Higher and higher the stranger led Stefa. Once a week he would take her for a brief ideological conversation with a group of ancient retired revolutionaries, fathers of the great Revolution. And nightly high and low he slavered over her body with an almost inaudible hissing.

Not alone.

In the small hours of the morning all the ancient revolutionaries clustered into her bed and inscribed slogans and redeeming notions on her white back with slobbering Cyrillic tongues. They clasped her waist with cold, purple-veined fingers, large dead nails of yellow tallow. They were toothless, most of them, and feverish, schooled in lubricity, steering their pleasures with cold stratagems, breathing faint odours and coarse odours in her face, moving methodically, crackling as if their skeletons had collapsed beneath their parchment-pale skins. She would wriggle, with muffled sobs, struggling in vain to kick and escape, the old men were weak but numerous and experienced, and all her efforts only served to inflame still further the swarming lascivious tangle, the sweat ran, the wallowing mêlée became more and more sticky, frothy, moaning, pierced intermittently by sharp, cruel screams. Between the bodies thick pungent juices squelched. They were so abandoned, those ancient fathers of the great Revolution; till daybreak they were not sated. Stefa sank slowly in the slimy slushy sewage, veins bulging ready to burst, uprooted grey hairs caught in her nails, solitary teeth straining to dig into her breast or her lower belly, sometimes wrenched from the rotting gums, dead lips stifling her lips and her sobs and her screams. Till daybreak.

But eventually it transpired that the stranger who had brought her here was in fact not tall, not thin or deadly, not even real.

An abstract form had come to Stefa. Not even a form. A theoretical possibility. A passing shadow. A nothing.

Cyrillic letters, lecherous fathers of the great Revolution, all these were really no more than twilight shades of a period of change.

So Stefa Pomeranz left Krasnoyarsk for Moscow. No more appraisals of the reliability of delicate playwrights, no more reports on professors who saw both sides of every question.

Here in Moscow Stefa was put in charge of political propaganda that was directly connected with the salvation of the new Poland. A small team was set up. A plan was approved. Certain people saw Stefa as a rising star. Others immediately accepted their opinion. All Stefa's

45

gifts, all her charms radiated a sense of perfect discretion and receptiveness.

Next winter, to an accompaniment of vodka and cymbals, Stefa was married in Moscow to a little spy master by the name of Fedoseyev. He was in charge of one of the secret departments, and a great future was prophesied for him too. He was a cold, blue-jawed man, whose beard no razor in the world could contain for longer than three hours. He was gloomy most of the time, in the Russian manner, he was forever loving beauty in all its forms—both in art and in nature—and he was also a good chess player. What disgusted Stefa more than all these things was his habit of secretively pursing his fleshy lips as if he were forever sucking a sour sweet and successfully exercising himself to conceal the fact.

Stefa and her team devised a comprehensive campaign. A close but unobtrusive watch was set on the Polish intelligentsia. Stefa would occasionally amuse herself by reading a photocopied love letter from some celebrated Marxist to a Martha Pinch-me-not, or listening to the broken whispers of two or three disappointed world reformers on a tape recorder. Some of these men were marched into her bureau in Moscow on their way to the vast developments in the northeastern regions of the Soviet State. It was in her power, sometimes, to spare one of them, in which case she would correct his misguided thinking, wag her finger at him like a schoolmistress, imprison him with one of her smiles, forgive him, and permit him to go back safely to Warsaw and justify her confidence in him. Once she even intervened on behalf of an ageing musicologist and released him when springtime came to go to his beloved Palestine. Once there, he hastened to send her a coloured picture postcard, some holy tomb, a Jewish soldier, and a pair of palm trees under an unimaginably blue sky. And he added in Polish : Be assured, Comrade, of the gratitude and blessing of a weary soul.

One night Stefa was invited to meet Stalin himself. Comrade Fedoseyeva had been praised by many for her large warm eyes, for her sweeping eyelashes, her overpowering smile. In addition, her work was considered by various comrades to be masterly, and Fedoseyev, too, had been mentioned with approval.

The conversation touched on the history of the kings of Poland, the complicated younger generation of intellectuals, the delusive influence exerted by things French on the exasperating Poles. Stalin served tea and honey cakes with his own hands, and suddenly began juggling with the sugar lumps like a little boy. It was a fascinating and amusing display of dexterity : one lump resting on Stalin's huge nicotine-stained thumbnail, another arching through the air, the two touching in mid-air and landing safely in Stefa's glass, splashing the scalding tea. Stalin roared and thundered : hee-hee, Comrade Fedoseyeva, that's something no Pole can do, such feats are beyond them, I'm willing to bet on it here and now, Comrade Fedoseyeva, and I can assure you, Comrade Fedoseyeva, you won't be the winner. Now have another glass of tea, my beauty, and then—forward march, you back to your work and I to mine, otherwise we'll both be arrested for flirting on duty. We'll just exchange a tiny kiss to release a little of our mighty passions. And Stefa said to herself : Look, without lifting a finger, almost without a smile, I'm making the Bear dance.

Stalin detained Stefa for a few minutes longer to tell her about the beautiful regions that he with his own hands had wrested from the Germans and served up to the Poles, to eat and relish till the fat ran down over their silly Polish chins. Stefa was advised to keep a close watch on all her friends, because only a fool or a Czech would trust a Pole, and that it would also be a wise precaution to keep an occasional eye on her own Fedoseyev, because he had blue eyes, as far as he could

47

remember, and a Russian with blue eyes was like a Jew with a straight nose : you never knew what he might get up to. As Stalin saw Stefa to the door and out into the corridor and said good night and nevertheless insisted on accompanying her downstairs, he once or twice pinched her cheek with a large-nailed thumb and forefinger. The Russians at that time still hung great hopes on the political enthusiasm of Polish Jews. And soon afterward they hung Fedoseyev too. In the course of a purge, that is.

And Stefa took his place, by special command.

From now on she had secret agencies at her disposal. Her task was to identify treacherous elements in various far-off places. And she said to herself : until I get hold of the Bear's skin.

13

Suddenly, in the course of an autumn in the late 'fifties, Pomeranz realized beyond all shadow of doubt that he was being followed, wherever he went, cunningly, silently, patiently.

His life was well ordered. Every morning, the paper, the news on the radio, a roll and cheese, halva, olives, coffee. Then a stern, almost angry shave. As if the mirror were water, not glass.

At eight o'clock, clutching a small briefcase, youthful in a blue shirt and sandals, he left his flat and walked down to the lower town to his shop opposite Aldubi's Garage, Automobile Parts and General Repairs. The town was at the mercy of the blazing morning. The white light tormented the lake. The ancient mountains stood, as always, unchanged. Pomeranz would note that their repose had endured yet another day.

In his shop he would switch on the fan, and fiddle

with the radio until he found some Greek music from Nicosia, then move on to listen to an ecstatic announcer on Radio Damascus, pass on again to settle on the wail of a muezzin, sad, forlorn, and yet tense with a veiled menace.

Every half hour or so he would stop, look up from his work, and stare out the window. Muscular, guttural men, amazing dark-skinned girls, handsome wolflike youths with a spring in their walk passed in front of his shop. Every now and again an old Jew would walk past, with a beard and sidelocks, and the youths would neither abuse him nor taunt him nor spit at him nor pull his beard. *Promised Land,* Pomeranz would say to himself: *pure and free.*

All morning a moderate breeze blew slyly from the east, as if sent by the mountains to collect and assemble specific facts and take them back to the mountain clefts. Here and there on the slopes up which the town of Tiberias spread there still grew a few ancient, gnarled olive trees, furiously sucking up buried juice with roots like hooked claws. Nothing was settled yet. Anything was possible.

Sometimes it was a young man with a slight hunch, who leaned against the wall of the Civic Centre on the corner of the street and smoked with a melancholy expression. An overcast, high-browed Raskolnikov. He watched Pomeranz enter and leave his house, and his protracted stares betrayed a certain loneliness.

When Raskolnikov disappeared, two men with sunglasses settled at one of the tables which spilled out on to the sidewalk from the café next to Aldubi's Garage. Pomeranz nicknamed both of them together Run-Jesus. Most of the time it seemed to him that they had a tendency to doze off at their post. A second glance, however, always revealed that only one of them was dozing, his head resting on one side, as if he were listening to faraway music, while his companion leaned his hairy forearms on the Formica tabletop, toying with a salt shaker, his eyes behind his sunglasses apparently fixed in a stare. He chewed his tongue with calm, devoted persistence.

Pomeranz could not imagine who might have sent these young men to keep watch on his comings and goings. Or what might be the purpose or the idea behind it.

Fear and sadness took hold of him; sudden doubts about the continuing efficacy of the secret powers which had preserved him during the bad years that had gone before.

From time to time, standing in his room, he happened to lean his elbows on the windowsill, and found it solid : wood and stone. As if after all these years the whispering current of energy had weakened and something in the outside world was gradually congealing. Massivity was spreading. Even his body was solidifying from within. His face, once that of a spy in an American comedy, had assumed a new expression : that of a tired old businessman troubled by financial worries. His mop of tawny hair was streaked with grey. He was being followed. Some secret organization. A hostile power had remembered all these years and now its agents had come to Tiberias. The cordon would never be slackened. Should he consider ways of escape, or, rather, take no notice?

Is there anyone here, man or demon, who has the power of taking off and floating over rooftops, fields, and meadows? The natural order here is earthly. You can belch to your heart's content, flail with your arms, play music, test your own skull with an axe, boast of your virgin birth till you're blue in the face, but the axe will be soft as rubber and the lake, for its part, will yawn indifferently in the savage midday sun : that's old hat, we've heard it all before, virgin birth, signs and wonders, gospels and persecutions, can't you think of something new. And don't try walking on the water, either.

The mouth organ, naturally, had long since rusted away.

A stern gravity reigns in these parts. No snow, no lunatic spires of village churches, no white steppes and black ravens, no howling wolves at night, no fir forests. The nights are quiet. Silence accumulates slowly. This is the Jordan Valley. And the lake at night is huddled and blind.

And so, like a man waking up in a panic and dashing for his life, Mieczyslaw the First suddenly started taking an interest in other people. Checking his longitude and latitude. Clinging. Getting to know. He ordered a daily newspaper. He bought a map of the roads and settlements. Made the acquaintance of his neighbours. Began to pat the dogs and children. Met a woman.

14

When Stefa recalled her former life, her youth, the intelligentsia of the town of M—— straining their fingertips to touch her with their ideas, when she recalled in the soft Russian sunshine how in a fit of caprice she had once suddenly given herself to the dreamy son of a mere watchmaker and how the town had buzzed with gossip and Emanuel Zaicek had whispered to her, In God's name, Stefa, you're throwing yourself away, when Stefa recalled how she used to touch the watchmaker's son on the forehead with her fingertip and touch their love and how her fingertip had lit up, when Stefa recalled all this she was seized by a mood of wild restlessness. Her heart yearned for savage sun-drenched places, feverishly she dispatched coded cables to Timbuktu, Barcelona, Pago Pago, Newfoundland, and New Caledonia, Mikhail Andreitch at her command would flash a short signal in cypher and at once an officers' conspiracy would get under way in Brazzaville or a strike of armed workers in Caracas.

Everybody, Stefa felt, every town and nation, we are all in need of urgent salvation, now, at once, how much more can we stand, the heart is ready to burst.

She would suddenly touch with her toe the flattened head of Mikhail Andreitch, who lay on the rug at her feet :

'Andreitch. Pay attention. Listen.'

(Moscow. Melting snow. Soft sunlight at the barred window.)

'I am listening, Comrade Fedoseyeva. I'm all ears.'

'Listening maybe, Andreitch, but you still can't hear. You don't hear a thing. The air is full and you—nothing. Delicate, amazing things are about to happen. Starting to stir. Turning over. So wake up, Andreitch, if you don't mind, stand on your own two feet, wake up. Stop listening and start hearing at long last.'

The office of the Chairman of the Sixth Bureau was a low-ceilinged but spacious room, furnished in an eccentric style. There was no desk. No shelves or chairs. Comrade Fedoseyeva was in the habit of working while lying on her back, with her knees drawn up, or else propping herself up on her side with her elbow. The principal item of furniture in her office was therefore a low divan in Central Asian style.

Next to the divan was a camel-hair rug, and it was on this that flat-headed Mikhail Andreitch crouched on guard. Two telephones without dials to his left, two flexible microphones to his right, and in front of him on a stool an ashtray, lighter, three or four packages of Sobranie cigarettes, and some small brightly coloured notebooks. On the wall hung a picture of the Bear in marshal's uniform, wearing a sleepy, satisfied smile.

There was also a samovar and two glasses. And an electric fire.

At first sight it was not easy to believe that from here invisible wires, nervous quivering piano wires, extended to four continents, with large numbers of men at the other end, different kinds of men, some of them remarkably sensitive and all of them, like all men, in need of urgent salvation. Could Comrade Fedoseyeva, with all her taut wires, her overpowering smile, bring about any illumination? Could she touch with her fingertip and see her fingertip light up?

She knew not where he was, she had no tears; and her hair was ruthlessly cropped.

From her window she could see amazing Slavic domes, pot-bellied domes, reaching up to heaven in a desperate effort to be freed from their bodies, to be touched by a north wind, to be wounded by the wind, to belong to the wind.

15

Pomeranz shaved off his thin, lovingly cultivated moustache, and for a time contemplated taking a Hebrew name : Miron Primor. Nonsense.

While round about him things closed in, even took a turn for the worse. Sometimes when he came home from work it happened that a long, curvaceous motorcar was parked on the corner of the street with some men inside it with their hats pulled down.

They made no effort to disguise their purpose.

As if they were certain that he had no possibility, no chance, no inclination to elude them and suddenly vanish. As if they knew the secrets of his own heart.

A kind of cheap comedy was closing in around him, and in addition to fear and sorrow he also felt disgust.

At night, as he sat at his desk working at his mathematical researches by the light of a small table lamp, he would suddenly be compelled to turn his head, and he would see shadow upon shadow. The newspaper, too, warned the watchful public to be on the alert against all sorts of dangers: keep an eye open, report anything suspicious at once.

And rest, if rest indeed it had been, was no longer to be had.

Even the stone-built house, with its low-vaulted ceiling and its window boxes aflame with geraniums, suddenly began to exude different smells. The arching movement of the ceiling could be sensed at night with ever-increasing force. A solitary tough stem sprouted through a crack in the flagstones near the kitchen alcove, and stood erect and stiff, holding up its lonely grey head. And a woman also appeared.

Petite, confused, American, a kind of free artist, liberation of style or of line. One Saturday morning she suddenly knocked at Pomeranz's door. Slender, straight as a twig, she smiled, she asked if she might sketch the arches, she was embarrassed yet bold, as she spoke she almost accidentally touched his arm, his shoulder, his cheek, she laughed, looked grave, she thought the walls were so old and expressive, such a simple harmony in the vaulting, and, oh, what an enchanting devil's head carved on the stone lintel, and the view of the palm trees through the arched window, those psychedelic flickers of light on the lake, contrasting with the grimness of the mountains, she wanted to sketch it all, and she promised not to make a mess or a noise, could she, please?

Yes, of course.

Audrey. All pink, blooming, full of zeal, full of ideas, touchingly slender, detached from her body, not too

54

clean, perhaps, even—Pomeranz was overcome by an ardent desire to forgive her, forgive her anything. She wore a kind of American Indian dress, and Rosa Luxemburg glasses. Her hair was dusty, unruly, at odds with itself. She was outrageously young. Barefoot. Her restless toes ceaselessly dug into the stone floor as if trying to burrow through and touch the earth beneath, a movement of curiosity or of orphaned frenzy.

For four days and five nights Audrey stayed with Pomeranz : he for the flavour of her body and she for the meaning of life. He would writhe, gurgle, struggle, death throes pierced the marrow of his bones every few hours, shimmering delusive spasms, axe blow, virgin birth. In between, Audrey barefoot roamed from window to window, glowing, adapting to captivity, like Adam in Paradise calling everything by a new name, taking up stands, formulating, pointing everything its way to renewal and salvation, expounding, connecting, legislating. All with her fingertips. As if she were dreaming.

In midstream, somewhere in a sentence that had begun with the death of God and would have led on to existential guilt, the man would pounce and seize her stemlike neck in his dark heavy-veined hands and contemplate for a moment its fragility, desperately inhaling all her odours, his hands two heavy slow cascades running down her back, her waist, he would sink into her hair, clasp her breasts, his preying hands full of spreading mercy.

Panting. Her silence. And his.

The widening gap between their silences.

And, after a few moments, the words again,
Audrey to Pomeranz :

National Liberation. International Liberation. Inner Liberation. What do you think. My generation, your generation. And also : Liberation of the body. Liberation from the restraints of the body. The other reality. Liberation through violence. All war is dereliction. The meaning of unfulfilled longing. The natural right to universal gratification. And also : Revolutionizing the Revolution. The Jew as a symbol. Revitalizing decay, uninvolved vitality. And also : Consistency, the modern neurosis. Drugs, a simple remedy. The purifying vigour stored up in the black race. Reason is a cancer. Reality, Audrey said, is a petit-bourgeois escape. The final revolution, Audrey said, will be a fantasy of sounds, an orgy of colours, the abolition of death.

Pomeranz casually pardoned these venial sins. He bent over her simple innocence, forced an entrance, plunged his red-hot loneliness into her. In between desperate pants he in turn began preaching to Audrey : The absurdity of gravity. The potency of high notes. Bugles. A Polish kingdom in the Aegean Islands. Music, which is audible mathematics.

And also : Sewing-machine parts. The branch of a chestnut tree which grew into the back of the bronze statue of Slowacki in Sobieski Square. Swiss promissory notes. The silence of the forest and the borderline between it and the silence of the low sky in winter. Village sorceresses, Prsywolski the Last, Mieczyslaw the First, anointed in exile with sewing-machine oil. The Princess Magda Isawolska, the Virgin Whore. Her sin and absolution. And also : Vampires. Thoughts like radar beams. And again : Music, the mysterious link between magnetism and electricity. As opposed to physical relations, the clumsy ephemeral convergence of abstract energies.

And finally : Vikings. Nibelungs. Pork fat.

As against : The song of the stars. Release from the body. Levitation. The power of love. The potency of grace.

In brief, what was there in common. He with his. She with hers. Another night, another day, perhaps another night. Not a line had she sketched here, but she had had an *Experience*. Now she would be on her way. 'Bye. And he lay back, astounded.

But he found no rest.

16

A new character knocked on the door.

A short, brisk middle-aged man, with remarkably short fingers, one eye smaller than the other, and his ears straining forward. Like a rabbi who for years has been secretly committing adultery. He was accompanied by three tall, handsome young men who all looked alike and collectively resembled the familiar representation of a young pioneer. Throughout the visit they displayed an extreme deference toward the senior visitor: they sat when he sat, stood when he stood, and were silent when he spoke. He was calling on behalf of the Central Intelligence Bureau. He had one or two questions to put and then he would be off: God Almighty preserve us from the sin of wasting other people's valuable time. Tiberias, incidentally, seemed to him to be losing its charm: all housing developments and eucalyptus trees. So sad. The lake, on the other hand, was a thing of beauty and a joy forever. After all, it was, up to a point, a historic lake. No, no tea, thank you, I am on duty, and I wish to cause you the minimum possible inconvenience. The boys won't have any, either: they're such magnificent lads, content with so little, almost spiritual, up to a point. Incidentally, a single man's lot is not a happy one. A married couple can offer each other mutual assistance, but a single man has no one to help him. There's a story told of Rabbi Levi Yitzhak of Berdichev which illustrates this perfectly —but there, we haven't come here to tell anecdotes,

57

only to put one or two questions and then be off. I myself am, up to a point, a single man too, but that is a horse of a different colour, and we must stick to the matter in hand. To return to the point, then. A single man must guard, above all else, against wallowing in self-pity. Self-pity is our worst enemy. The topic can be reinforced by a trivial example from my own professional work. For some time now we have been put to enormous trouble investigating a certain foreign agent, an elusive, cunning, Communist, dangerous Infidel by the name of Stravinsky, alias Davidson, alias the Siberian, alias Father Nicodeme. Well, to cut a long story short, whatever his real name, this agent is apparently the centre of a number of radiating spokes. A kind of outspread net, in other words. It is a flattering state of affairs, is it not, if we adopt a certain point of view. At the risk of exaggerating, one might almost say a source of natural, justifiable pride, that we excite their curiosity to such an extent. That they honour us by sending us a secret agent of the first water, so to speak, a real expert, a virtuoso soloist, if I may borrow a metaphor from the realm of the arts to serve our own, which is that of vulgar melodrama. In other words, they already regard us as worthy of their serious attention. Into a pail you don't throw a whale, to coin a phrase. But that is not the crux of the topic, which is this : assuming that we are not—heaven forbid—following a false trail, it would appear that this Stravinsky is taking a close interest in a certain Pomeranz. Both the problem and its solution, as the Talmud so often teaches us, are contained in the same text. However our opinions may be divided on some matters, such as prophetic justice or life after death, in this case all five of us are bound to agree at once and beyond all shadow of doubt that a small question, a natural question, arises here : why should the aforementioned Father Nicodeme take such a lively interest in a mere master watchmaker from Tiberias? What is this, a comedy? Some kind of a joke?

Why should a Russian spy of the highest rank keep his beady eye on a very excellent watchmaker from Tiberias? Come, let us leave aside the practical aspect for a moment; after all, we are not half-witted blinkered bureaucrats out of a story by Gogol. Let us contemplate the topic from a broad theoretical stand-point. On a purely theoretical plane, the interest shown by this so-called Siberian in a man like yourself is a phenomenon calling for concentration and a penetrating mind. It excites the curiosity, like a game of chess, if we may be permitted the allusion in present company. In other words, a man's private life is his own affair. *Da.* Very well. But perhaps, nevertheless, something did happen to you in Europe? Europe is, in a sense, a very important continent for us. Words of mine can hardly do justice to the importance of Europe. *Alors,* my dear sir, do try to remember. Make an effort. Please. You were in Vienna, were you not? And in Athens. You spent some time in Piraeus. You must have seen some splendid sights. You are a man of the world, as they say. Well? No, wait, excuse me, why the haste? Don't be in too much of a hurry to answer. Such matters merit leisurely reflection, concentration, perhaps a certain amount of caution; they should be regarded as rather delicate matters. What is more, the climate is decidedly hot today. Why don't we relax for a moment, forget about these burning issues, and exchange stories and anecdotes. Why was it that at the beginning of February you decided to purchase a map of the roads and settlements? After all, you are not, if one may say so, a geographer, but a mathematical personality, up to a point. Mathematics, incidentally, is, to my mind, a sublime and precious member of the family of the sciences, if a mere simpleton may be permitted to express a personal opinion. And Fedoseyeva, my dear sir, what does the name Fedoseyeva mean to you? Yes, indeed, it is a Russian name. Distinctly Russian. After all, we are all of us Russian—unless of course we happen to be Polish.

59

By the way, you studied under Professor Emanuel Zaicek, a fascinating personality, not only in the field of philosophy but also in the dissemination of new ideas. After all, we now know beyond all shadow of doubt, we have examined, tested, and proved, we have tirelessly fitted one detail to another, we know that you hail from the same town originally as a certain member of the Cabinet. So many fine threads come together to weave a broad, fascinating fabric. You come from the same town as one of our Cabinet ministers, you are a pupil of a brilliant professor, you are the darling of a Communist agent of the first water, and to cap it all you are also a mathematical celebrity, who out of an excess of modesty has chosen to settle in a remote country town and repair tiny watches—only a fool would underestimate all these various advantages. *Da.* To the heat we might eventually manage to get acclimatized, but this humidity turns every human being into a running fountain of perspiration. And what of the tourist girl? Was it pure chance that brought her here—to Israel of all countries, to Galilee of all regions, to Tiberias of all towns, to this house of all possible places? Wasn't she on a mission? Or was there no ulterior purpose, simply divine guidance? Was this same young lady not recently the girl friend of a black radical leader in New York, which is a gigantic city in the full sense of the word? Well, we must not meddle in affairs of the heart, *nyet,* never, as a matter of principle. The young lady stayed with you, and that's that. This is a matter of the emotions up to a point, of physical attraction, love, et cetera; we are not experts in this field, and we lack the professional qualifications to deal with such a subject. On the contrary. To come back to the matter in hand. It would be rather exciting, even somewhat nostalgic, if you would be kind enough—for the purpose of purely theoretical comparison—to show us your old passport. From those days. No, do you take us for imbeciles, we do not of course desire to see a genuine passport; we are not so indiscreet. Look here, I'll let you into a confidence, just between ourselves and absolutely off the record : even a forged passport is enough to excite men of our profession. We are modest in our demands, my dear Przywolski, we represent a poor nation, no one supports us with training and funds, like the Goethe Society or your clever gang in Piraeus. By the way, can any Jew worthy of the name lay claim to a genuine passport? In those days even we ourselves were not above stealing across a little border or two here and there with the assistance of forged papers. After all, those were days of troubles and incomplete security, as we both know so well. These charming young men, on the other hand, who are such a feast for the eyes, what do they know, what can they understand of those days? I pride myself on the love of literature, the love of knowledge which I have implanted in their breasts. That is why they are now leafing through your notebooks and papers—without, heaven forbid, creating any disorder—and if you have no objection perhaps they might also peep into your desk drawers. With your kind permission, of course. Nature reigns supreme on mountain, vale, and stream. Let's go back to those old days. At that time twilight offered almost the only hope. Provided you had documents drawn up by a loving and also professional hand. Coincidentally, Father Nicodeme, with whom we began our little conversation, and whose attention you have attracted to yourself, is also suspected of having Polish origins. And again, to pile coincidence on coincidence, you were not born to be a watchmaker, were you? A horse pulls a cart, and doesn't try to be too smart. Just between ourselves, my dear sir, you are a scientist, are you not, a scholar, a maker of discoveries. We unearthed a brilliant piece of work by you in *Kulturny* for March, 1938, about time, gravity, and magnetic fields, work which I am informed represents a small step beyond Einstein, and now we suddenly find you tinkering with clocks and watches. How come, I ask myself. And you yourself admitted ten minutes ago that you are secretly engaged in various kinds of researches or studies, and experiments, would you agree that curiosity naturally burns within us like a strong flame, how could you bear to abandon your wife to the mercy of the Germans and make your escape alone, and why did you pick on a quiet remote spot like Tiberias, of all places, such an innocent spot, and where did you get a hold of the money you brought with you, and why watches, and who sent the young American lady to you, and what is the connection between you and Fedoseyeva, why is Father Nicodeme so eager to know your movements, and who – if I may be permitted to intrude into your more intimate affairs – who was it who financed the Goethe Society in the town of M——in the days of the Polish Republic, and what was behind the respectable façade of that philosophical society, that is to say, who gave Professor Zaicek his orders, and who in turn gave you yours? And who else from that group, apart from yourself and the Cabinet minister I have mentioned, has succeeded in reaching this country, and all in all—I ask myself in amazement, in exasperation almost—how does it come about that a brilliant Jewish scientist, physicist, and researcher such as yourself suddenly and simply leaves German-occupied Poland, just like that, as if it were nothing, as if you could build a wall out of nothing at all, to coin a phrase. The whole business gives us no rest, as you can understand, it has all been checked and supported by documents, photographs, and fingerprints, and we have several options open to us if we decide to examine you closely. A Jew sets out one fine day, leaves occupied Poland just like that, and flits backward and forward between Vienna and Budapest, Bucharest and Piraeus, instead of heading straight for his homeland, and he a scientist, who must have a few juicy tidbits about him, and then he shuts himself away up here like a paragon of modesty and self-effacement, how does it come about, I ask myself, and for how much longer. So you see, Fedoseyev, questions, questions, and still more questions, and I have already told you that these beautiful young men are simply mad about literature : they would sacrifice their own mothers for the sake of a good story. So if the four of us meet with your approval, let's all smoke a cigarette together, and why don't you, of your own free will, tell them a nice appetizing story? Admittedly you are addressing a very limited audience. One might even say an intimate audience. A drawing-room audience. On the other hand, it is a hand-picked audience. Even I, who am no artist, receive their whole-hearted attention. By the way, before we hear the story, we should very much like to know the author's name, so that we can give credit where credit is due. What is your name, Pomeranz?

17

There is a desolate place on the bank of a sluggish stream, where three ancient, ailing lemon trees silently grow without hope or reason, as though the sun has gone out. The dying trees are being slowly strangled by the lush growth all around. Not a sound. The light is tired and strange, beyond day or night. Even the river lapping at its bank is mute. The thick vegetation, tall enough to hide a man, from time to time exudes ripples of vague smell. The smell is rank, lusty, almost fetid.

Not a bird could there be here. Not a fish in the stream, not a beast in the thicket. Only distant crickets occasionally testing their strength and at once despairing. No movement, no breeze. And here is Emanuel Zaicek, his skin brown and scorched, the bear's skin wrapped round his shoulders, his white beard unkempt. He is kneeling on all fours, drinking or kissing the water. He is alone.

18

A new leaf : Pomeranz easily guessed the identity of the woman Fedoseyeva, was almost certain of that of Father Nicodeme, and was thus in a position to place the Cabinet minister beyond all suspicion. He also took an oath of loyalty to the State of Israel and gave his word of honour to restrict his activities to his own domain, so as not to encroach on that of others and so give rise to another false alarm. The authorities would agree in return to leave him in perfect peace, and guarantee his private status.

He left his apartment and his work, closed up his shop and sold the fittings. He spent some days touring the villages, following his map of the roads and settlements. In a few places he even worked some minor rustic wonders, like flexing a small muscle : tricks of legerdemain at a pound a time, seventy agorot for children. But he soon abandoned even these tours, because his heart pleaded for final rest.

So the time came for a new, almost idyllic reincarnation, a kind of virgin birth. Pomeranz had finally prepared himself for working on the land. He took his leave of Tiberias and settled in a kibbutz in Upper Galilee. As a man turns from side to side in his sleep. He accepted the job of shepherd, and agreed to repair watches whenever necessary. His mop of hair was turning grey, and the thick bushes above his small eyes were growing silvery. His face had become that of a saint in a rustic icon. Still the same powers of adaptation, as clinging as ivy.

Pomeranz settled down behind a wall of quietude. Day resembled day and night repeated night. There was a slow, deliberate routine, as if he intended to prove that he could bathe in the same river twice, or even once. All fuss he hated heartily. People, scenes, and ideas flowed past him, and he sat quietly, saying nothing.

Once they tried to make him participate, to co-opt him on to a small committee, the Garden Committee. But he, with his pensive smile, with his autumnal manners, asked them to leave him in peace. He already repaired their watches, and took the sheep out to pasture every day, he was meticulously regular with the milking and feeding and cleaning the stables; if they wanted him to he would willingly give some coaching in science to the slow learners. But he begged them not to press him. And he redoubled his silence.

If ever he recalled his wife, what he remembered was not the music of her voice but her hair, her fragrance, and her tears. And he would see as from a great distance the late afternoon light slowly fading in Jaroslaw Avenue, and the street lights coming on one by one, as if unwillingly marring the colour of the night. He saw Stefa, slender, silhouetted against the parapet of the bridge, smoking with her back to him. He himself standing four paces behind her, smoking slowly. And just beneath their feet the river and the bridge, making no concession or allowance, ceaselessly flowing in two conflicting directions, and the two crossed streams were love.

In his large hands he remembered Audrey. At times the memory came as an obstinate stirring. He would concentrate, think music, cling to the music like a man clinging to a high balustrade, and after a while he would be able to laugh at himself. Other memories he could not vanquish so easily, could not vanquish at all, must give up the struggle. Float downstream. Close himself up and suffer in silence.

In his leisure hours Pomeranz would sit alone in his kibbutz room—wardrobe, bed, lampshade, table, cloth, and vase—setting himself and solving various algebraic equations and mathematical puzzles. Outside his window could be seen neat ranks of kibbutz flowers planted in the clefts of the rocks and assiduously tended. Further on, on the slopes of the hill, stood a few young, enthusiastic cypress trees, apparently in a perpetual state of ecstasy. Further still, beyond the wadi, he could see a grey mountainous landscape, boulders, olive trees, and wind. And over all midday silence or night breeze.

Among the members of the kibbutz his face, the face of an exiled Russian poet or Orthodox saint, caused a certain puzzlement, almost amounting to public perplexity, but his face had the power of preserving his privacy.

School children who had difficulty in learning would come to him two or three evenings a week. He had volunteered to give them some extra tuition in science. Occasionally there would be a sudden flash of illumination. One of the greasy-haired, nail-biting, acne-ridden louts would suddenly grasp Pythagoras's theorem, and his normally blank eyes would light up for a brief instant. Or one of the frivolous, flighty girls would inhale Pomeranz's smell with nervous, quivering nostrils and suddenly her eyes would be opened and she would see an integral. There was also a large, miserable dog, perhaps half-jackal, who shared Pomeranz's room. He had come to the kibbutz from nowhere, out of the night, an old, worn-out, thoroughly apathetic creature. Or he may have been melancholic.

Some people said :

'That Elisha, he's a real brain. We ought to bring him out of himself. He's a human being, he's one of our own members, and he's destroying himself in front of our very eyes.'

Others said :

'Oh, really. Why don't you just let him be.'

Or worse :

'No wonder, after everything he must have been through.'

There were others who said :

'He belches at night. In Polish. Or perhaps he's talking. Talking in the night to that dog of his, which isn't even a dog really.'

And finally they said :

'It's a case for the nurse. We're not living in the jungle.'

19

Stretched out as usual on her carved divan from Turkestan or Bukhara, Comrade Fedoseyeva dictated various instructions concerning Palestine to her principal assistant, lying below her on the rug :

'We need to put out a few feelers in Palestine, Mikhail Andreitch, there you are again fast asleep like Plekhanov, something is going to happen any moment now in Palestine.'

Mikhail Andreitch wriggled quickly on the camel-hair rug by the side of the low divan, raised his flat head toward Comrade Fedoseyeva, bared his teeth, sharpening yet further his habitual expression of perpetual thirst, and defended himself palely :

'What is Palestine, Comrade Fedoseyeva? Palestine is nothing. Nothing at all. A few small colonies. A few oranges. A few holy ruins. Foreign capital. Immigration. A bit of shooting once or twice a week. The whole thing on a Lilliputian scale. No bigger than your little finger. Palestine is nothing, Comrade Fedoseyeva.'

Stefa :

'But they're always making new discoveries, formulae, inventions, a wonder cure for cancer they say they've found there only they're keeping it secret from the outside world so as to raise the price, and there have been some atomic rumours, secret weapons they're developing there by night, and as for you, Andreitch, you're just like the mujik who looked through the telescope and said, It's nothing, it's nothing. Your kind were no ordinary people, your kind were barons once, generals, governors of big towns, they used to go whish through the air with their whips in those days. Now concentrate, Andreitch dear, think hard, try to make amends and tell Mother sensibly and intelligently what they've got in Palestine.'

Mikhail Andreitch, with a look of stupid panic on his thirsty face, his grin broadening to that of a terrified cat, his teeth short and white :

'Don't, Comrade Fedoseyeva, please don't, you know that kind of talk won't help either of us, the past is all behind us now and our faces are turned to the future. Look, I am thinking, I'm thinking quickly and thoroughly. I'm thinking full steam ahead, if there is such an expression.'

'And your conclusion, my dear *Stakhanovich*?'

'Conclusion. Yes, conclusion. Where could we be without conclusions. Well, yes. Palestine it is, Comrade Fedoseyeva : I'm ready to pack my bags and go, if those are your orders. I'll go anywhere you like without a murmur. But still, Palestine is a rather unimportant spot. And tiny. A kind of temporary refugee camp that our Jews have set up among the sand dunes and holy ruins. They're still trying to get their bearings, everything there is still in a confused, experimental stage.'

Fedoseyeva :

'That will do, Andreitch. It's not for theoretical arguments that I've been raising you here. Shut up, my peerless Andreitch. Shut up in Russian. Just make yourself a note : Palestine. You ought to be glad; I was certain you'd be writhing with joy. Palestine is full of nuns of every shape and size. But just you keep your hands off them. You can feast your eyes on them to your heart's content, but kindly keep your filthy paws to yourself. By the way. I suppose you've got some good men there who know a thing or two?'

'Yes, Comrade Fedoseyeva, I have indeed. And they're always complaining. They complain about the climate, they complain about the boredom, the language, and the flies. After all, it—how should I say—it isn't a very big place.'

'That's enough, Andreitch, you've said quite enough already. Now go and change, pack your overnight bag, and off you fly. Wait a minute.'

'Yes. Right away.'

'Stand still and stop jumping up and down. Now listen carefully. Apart from the nuns, the music there, I hear, is of the highest quality. Concerts, symphonies, Jews playing and singing with gusto—you won't be at a loss in Palestine. Prick your ears up, Andreitch. There's something in the air. You know better than anyone my sudden flashes of intuition. So don't fall asleep, Mikhail Andreitch. Things happen in Palestine.'

20

Elisha Pomeranz led a quiet life.

Sometimes in the evenings he fell prey to hesitations, and he, in his usual patient way, almost loved this moment. The burial of the last light of day. Noman and silence upon the broad lawns. Noman in the gardens.

Among the lilacs. The woods empty and shadow-soaked. A faint breeze blowing off the hills, touching the pines with its fingertips, coaxing them, spreading amazing rumours, whispering high limpid forgiveness. The breeze inspired the pines with a powerful quiet hallucination which was almost more than they could bear. Then, holding his breath, he could see with his own eyes the pine trees in the darkness stretching upward to the very bounds of music.

Afterward, by the light of mathematical theory or astronomical calculations: the intricate powers of circularity, radiating bodies in dark space, the opposing energies coursing between the bodies in curves which cannot be perceived by the senses, only by an abstract intention, until the intention suddenly casts doubt, almost ridicule, on the material objects round about. The shelf and its shadow. The desk. The lamp and its pool of yellow light. The paper. The pen. The rustling of the paper. His writing hand. The smell of his body. His body. His breath. The absurd connection between his calculations and the network of white threads, grey fluids, moisture, what a ridiculous connection. And so humiliating.

In short, the dreamy son of a watchmaker rendered unto the kibbutz those things which belonged to the kibbutz, and when he had completed all his labours he always closed himself up in his room and his silence.

The kibbutz, however, went on living its rhythmical life: day succeeded day, and the intervening nights were suppressed, because night always seems to be full of malign intentions and so it must be uncompromisingly shut out or cautiously circumvented. *No alternative.* Indeed, here among the rocky Galilean hills, where thorns flourished even on bare rocks, the nights certainly betrayed a threatening, simian quality.

Day succeeded day, and by seven o'clock white non-light already beat down on roofs and treetops, scorching

70

concrete paths, dominating deserted lawns, blazing on tiles and corrugated iron. The tyrannical light painted sharp clear circles round every enclave of shadow. Just so far. The frontiers of shade. Blue light. Line. White light. Line. Blue-white light. Square-cut hedges, neat rows of trees, tidy lawns, all speaking an unambiguous language. *Climb the mountains, crush the plain, All you see—possess it.* The tractor shed here, the dining hall there, and the recreation hall plugging the valley with its low, broad bulk. We are here. Guarding order. *Darkness to expel.*

Various suspicions were levelled at Pomeranz:
His peculiar indifference to the customary ideals.
His avoidance of all organized activities.
His lackadaisical attitude toward the betterment of Society and the Individual.
He doesn't read the evening paper even when you ram it under his nose.
He never makes suggestions.
Never criticizes.
You can never tell, with him.
Thinking. Who knows what.
So withdrawn.
How come?

The pupils he coached in the evening said:
'His room is always clean and spotless. It's a mania with him, tidiness. Whenever you try to sit down, he adjusts the angle of the chair to the table. If you accidentally kick up the corner of the rug, he goes down on all fours at once, like a long thin dog, and straightens it under your feet.'
'He keeps the lights dim, and there's always coffee and flowers in the room, and also a sort of faint smell everywhere which isn't the smell of the flowers or the smell of the coffee and you really can't tell what it is. Perhaps not a smell at all. Something. The air is differ-

ent in his room.'

'As if he's always expecting a special visitor.'

'And that silence. Even when he talks to you, it's as if he's talking in silence.'

'He's not all there. A bit gaga.'

'It can't go on. There's something strange about him, something lonely, how to put it, weird, it might be dangerous or something. Almost. Something might happen one day, all of a sudden. We ought to do something about him. Before it's too late.'

'And that dog. It's not a dog—it's a ghost.'

'It's frightening.'

So too, each evening, sitting on green benches under the lilac trees or on the edge of the lawn on deck chairs, the old women knitted Pomeranz. Wondering. Comparing. Remembering things that had happened and phrases from lectures or from the newspapers. Exchanging views and rumours. Pausing on a significant detail. Energetically well-meaning. Muttering a special salvation for him. A solution. Something.

Moreover, his name was included on the agenda of one of the kibbutz committees, a discreet item. Nothing urgent, though, nothing that couldn't be postponed.

Among themselves the other sheep farmers sometimes nicknamed Elisha Pomeranz 'the Wizard.' But the sheep, as ever, as in bygone days, since time immemorial, silently went on dreaming.

21

Soon or late, one clear pale night, Elisha Pomeranz arose and went down to the faraway waters to the thicket and the reeds to Emanuel Zaicek's hiding-place. He barely touched the ground as he went. He wore his pointed hat and his red boots, and his axe was tucked in his broad sash.

And when the two watchmakers' sons met on the bank of the stream they did not speak words or compare ideas or try to formulate a letter or a manifesto. For a while they both played the same Jewish melody on two different instruments; then they exchanged instruments and tried another similar melody. There was no breeze. The night was silent.

So they exchanged melodies.

Eventually Pomeranz reached up to the sky with a long bony arm and a transparent hand, pushed the moon aside and scattered a handful of stars over the darkening disc. Then he turned and went his way in peace into the clasp of the distant cricket song into the heart of the jackals' howling in the mountains.

22

Ernst, the Secretary of the Kibbutz Council, occasionally used to say :

'There's no smoke without a fire—the proverb presumably knows what it's talking about and who am I to pick a quarrel with an ancient proverb, but on the other hand the proverb doesn't say that whenever there's a fire the smoke has to appear at once or indeed at any stage whatever.'

(Ernst was in the habit of saying this or something like it whenever in the course of a meeting or debate anyone was carried away and restorted to excessively emotional arguments.)

Then something happened.

Elisha Pomeranz, a modest, retiring shepherd living in a kibbutz in the north of the country, has unexpectedly published an important article in a leading foreign scientific periodical. The article is by no means modest or insignificant : according to the headlines in the evening newspapers he has succeeded in solving one of the most baffling paradoxes connected with the mathematical concept of infinity.

It was a sensational event. The newspapers even told of the storm of excitement in the most remote centres of learning. Generations upon generations of scholars had broken their heads against the paradoxes of mathematical infinity, had muttered about the limitations of the human mind, had trembled as their thoughts tentatively probed the utmost limits of knowledge and encountered the frosty depths of the universe, adopted a tone of resignation in the face of the silence of eternal mysteries, and had always concluded : thus far and no farther. No one could ever cross this final line without collapsing into contradiction, absurdity, mysticism, ecstasy, or madness. This line marked the final limit of reason and the threshold of silence.

And now, to universal astonishment, a simple amateur, an outsider, working alone in a remote, out-of-the-way village, with the aid of nothing but pencil, paper, and solitude, had probed and hunted and suddenly come up with—

—an astounding theorem.

—a simple solution.

—a crystal-clear answer.

—breathtaking.

Not long afterward a gleaming black car drew up outside the hut which housed the kibbutz office. From it emerged a pair of elegantly dressed men. They were sinisterly alert. They inquired where they could find Pomeranz, if indeed such a man existed and he was not merely a trick or a delusion.

Ernst told them that at that time of day he was generally to be found in the pastures, and to the pastures they both disappeared at once in their black car. They were both well groomed, ostentatiously fresh looking, with wide American ties held in place by fine silver clips, and at the same time there was something daring about the cut of their suits, they wore cowboy-style belts or something of the sort and here and there there was a faint touch of the bohemian about them.

The determined visitors searched around for Pomeranz but they did not find him, because he was sometimes in the habit of taking his flocks across the wadi into the tangle of shallow gulleys, or up the rocky slopes among the boulders into the shady recesses of the olive plantation. The entire landscape, hills and valleys, the bluish mountains on the horizon, the hayfields in the plain, everything was veiled in a slight mist, and there was not a soul to be seen.

Alert man A said to alert man B :

'He's set the whole world buzzing and now he's lost somewhere in this goddam silence.'

Alert man B displayed a cautious smile, replaced it and answered :

'As soon as you said silence, goddam silence, I could hear the sound of an animal, a barking perhaps, and there's a rythmic throbbing noise on the other side of this hill.'

While they were talking in the open country, waiting, leaning on their magnificent car, pink and clean-shaven, exuding an air of infinite prospects and possibilities, bursting with arrogant, energetic enthusiasm, shattering the calm of the hills and plains by their very presence, devising their strategy and rehearsing the division of roles in the forthcoming conversation, while they lay in wait for Elisha—at that moment the telephone in the kibbutz office began ringing repeatedly and incessantly. Excited voices inquired indefatigably who he was and what he was like, what his weaknesses and his hobbies were, what his timetable was, when could they meet him, get to know him, make friends with him, interview him, chat with him, et cetera. Some of them were confident and blustering, some were honey-sweet, some were foreign, there were the skinny, bitter women of the international press, and wheedling women, a vast multitude. Nor was there any end to the flood of letters asking for advice, ideas, autographs, solutions, engagements, special tiny favours, and above all for usable photographs of Elisha Pomeranz against a background of fields or vineyards. Urgently: the whole world was standing and holding its breath, and time was of the essence.

23

In the thickly wooded basin of the Black Country to the north of the town of M—— there stands a tiny hamlet. It appears as though it can only exist by favour of the dense forest which seems to have made a momentary concession, to have opened up slightly to yield a small patch of plainland and a winding length of stream, an old wooden bridge, and once again closed in round about.

At the foot of this hamlet spreads a green meadow where cows graze in everlasting peace. Hay wains groan their way like pregnant women up the hill, struggling in the black mire. Beside them walk peasants carrying pitchforks, and they lend a shoulder as the need occurs.

In the middle of the hamlet among the dingy crooked hovels runs a mild, hesitant stream. The time is mid-afternoon: three o'clock or perhaps four. By the side of the stream sits a lean angler, bent forward. He has been sitting here since early morning, since before sunrise. His rod has fallen asleep in his hand, he has a hat made of folded newspaper on his head, his blue eyes stare blankly at the water, the hills, the forest opposite. His pose expresses idiocy, as does his fixed stare; his mouth gapes, a drop hangs from the tip of his nose, his lower jaw sags. The old man is as blank as a wall, but the plains the forest the stream all flow fearlessly all day long into his eyes and find room enough within.

On the opposite bank dusty peasant women with headscarves and spreading skirts chew endlessly on mint leaves or quids of tobacco and shoot out jets of yellow juice. They move on all fours, scratching potatoes out of the ground. And all the time, without the slightest whisper, the low grey sky arches oppressively over the hamlet and meadow. The small church reaches up on tiptoe toward the sky with its two towers, one ruined, the other unfinished. The church is entirely built of thick, blackening boards, and since it leans toward the south on account of the strong northerly winds it is propped up with four roughhewn slanting logs. The nails which once held them in place have long since rusted away, and the church is supported by inertia, equilibrium, exhaustion.

In front of the church there extends a small, rough-paved square, sagging toward the middle. When the building finally falls the square will enfold the remains and weeds will sprout up between the flagstones to consume everything in oblivion.

On the edge of the square a pair of ancient horses stand motionless, like statues from an equestrian group whose riders have been hacked off in the course of some political upheaval or change of heart. But the two horses, however old, are still alive. And motionless.

And now :

A girl, in the distance, almost a child, running, her hair struggling in the wind, perhaps crying silently, yes crying silently, running, clutching something, the distance and the grey light make it impossible to tell what, she trips, stumbles, falls flat, springs up again at once, surely panting, running, surely desperate, running toward the glimmering hills on the farthest horizon, too late, hopeless, running—

The whole scene is ruthlessly dominated by the reek of

wet hay, the stench of rotting fish, and a damp noxious vapour rising from the stream.

In a pool of mire stands a thin man leaning on one crutch, and Stefa watches wide-eyed as he brandishes the other furiously at the forest, at the sky, curses, describes intricate arabesques in the air, crosses himself fervently, wheels round, drops both crutches, and collapses into the mire.

Finally the rain comes:

Fine and piercing, whispering on damp hovels, scratching at their roofs, gently lashed by the northerly wind. Gradually the hills darken, straining wearily toward the water. A distant train lets out a shriek of horror. There is no bird here. Not even a raven.

And the Polish forest all around, ceaselessly hissing.

24

One Friday afternoon, after the end of the week's work and at the onset of twilight, when the air was full of recorder music from the children's houses and a smell of rain wafted among the small whitewashed buildings, Ernst, the Secretary, came to Pomeranz's room, accompanied by two middle-aged women. This time they came not with axes, mercifully, not with sneezing-powder, but with flowers. The middle-aged women thrust a graceful bunch of blazing yellow chrysanthemums into a vase. Their hands were thick-veined and weary.

'Shabbat Shalom,' said Ernst.

'Shabbat Shalom and good evening,' said the middle-aged women.

Pomeranz said:

'And the same to you. Won't you sit down?'

Ernst was a heavily built man in his sixties, with rather sagging features which inspired trust and friendship, yet whose expression did not try to conceal the doubts, the caution which were the fruit of disappointments and troubling experiences. Ernst also had remarkably thick grey eyebrows, one of which— the left one—was always slightly raised : Ernst was really amazed at you—how on earth could you have done such a thing to him. He was a man of experience, he would not waste words, he would merely raise one eyebrow in amazement and you, rebuked and embarrassed, would start apologizing incoherently in an attempt to placate that one raised eyebrow. In vain.

Ernst produced a small greeting card in a white envelope and put it on the table, under the vase. Then, in a slow, measured voice, he said :

'We have come on our own behalf and on behalf of the whole kibbutz family.'

Meanwhile the stray dog, the fox, watched from the corner of the room with quivering nostrils and sad veiled eyes. This creature was the terror of the children; he was almost always panting and growling, sometimes breaking out into a loud howl, he was virtually incapable of producing an honest bark, his drooping fur was a sickly grey. He looked like a stuffed dog.

Dziobak Przywolski, fresh and lively, just out of the shower and wearing a brown dressing gown, his jowl radiating a smell of shaving and towels, acknowledged the Secretary's opening gambit with a nod of the chin. He indicated a pair of chairs and an armchair. When his visitors were seated, he straightened the tablecloth and smoothed a slight crease in the bedspread. He was short and agile. There was not the slightest sign to be detected anywhere in the room of discoveries or inventions. There were a few volumes in English and German. Ernst squinted at them for a moment, as if their bindings might betray a clue to some misdemeanor which took place here when there was no one about to watch. Pomeranz picked up the envelope, opened it, briefly scanned the message—congratulations from the whole kibbutz family, your joy is our joy, on to ever greater things in the future—and broke his silence to ask:

'What joy?'

They said:

'The whole world is buzzing. Yesterday and this morning they were filming the life of the kibbutz.'

And they said:

'Such a discovery brings enormous benefit to the State of Israel.'

Pomeranz said nothing.

The guests found nothing to add, either.

There was a slight embarrassment, silence, an effort to smile.

Pomeranz carefully selected an orange, and opening the desk drawer on which his visitors' eyes were expectantly fixed he took out a knife, described an almost perfect circle at the top end and cut six amazingly precise lines of longitude down to the South Pole, where they all unerringly converged. After this performance the orange apparently peeled itself, in accordance with six slight hints. He opened it, carefully removed the pith, separated the segments, arranged them symmetrically on a glass plate as if bent on adding a chrysanthemum of his own to the bunch in the vase, and proffered it to his guests.

Ernst thanked him. The middle-aged women thanked him. Each of them took a segment, in order, from left to right. Pomeranz helped himself to one, following the same order.

Then one of the middle-aged women summoned up her resolution and spoke. She wanted to know, or at least to understand, how one could discover something scientific without test tubes, without flasks and retorts, at least some sort of equipment, without any . . . surely scientists always worked in special laboratories, she had once visited her nephew at the Weizmann Institute and she had seen, everybody there was wearing white coats, and anyway, surely . . .

Suddenly, in the middle of her question, she was struck by a thought. She decided to stop.

Pomeranz switched on the table lamp; the shadows were stirred up for a moment, and then regained their balance. And settled down. How calm the room was. How soft the tones of the curtains. The rug, two well-defined, simple colours. The patient bookshelves. The table. The four matching chairs. The single armchair. No ornaments or pictures. And in the corner facing the window another vase, a large tall one with some pine branches in it. Beside the door another low table, with the tea and coffee things on it. The grey bedspread. A slight quivering movement underneath it : the tip of the doglike creature's snout.

At the end of the silence, Ernst decided to light his pipe and come to the point. Well then, apart from congratulations and celebration there were also a few practical matters which it would be as well to talk over at some opportune moment, and in fact why not at this moment, which was in no way less opportune than any other. So. That morning the Farming Committee had debated the subject. It had been decided, on a motion proposed by Vera and carried unanimously, that young Shaulik, Yehuda Yatom's son, should be transferred to the sheep as from next week, so as to replace Elisha—at least part of the time, at this stage—and leave him free to devote two or possibly three mornings a week to his scientific researches.

Then Ernst put a question. Wreathed in tobacco smoke, slightly suspicious, looking like a man who feels a sudden slight pain. He wished to know if there was any kind of help the kibbutz could offer.

And raising his left eyebrow he explained :

'Material or otherwise.'

Pomeranz summoned up words. He was grateful for their kind attention, he was grateful for their good will, he was grateful for all their greetings. No, for the moment he could not think of anything he needed. But perhaps they would permit him to think it over for a day or two. Springtime was approaching, the sky was brightening, something might change at any moment.

The Secretary, after a minute's reflection, offered another proposal. He hesitated to put the question, he would have liked to be more certain of the answer first, but how would Elisha feel about the idea of giving a lecture to the other members about his discovery. Not, of course, a fully detailed, scholarly exposition, there was no need for the whole apparatus, but perhaps just a general, popular explanation, so that they would all know what it was about. In the broadest of outlines, naturally. After all, for most of the members modern science was more or less a new form of hieroglyphics. Would he let them have, how should he put it, a very general impression, enough to satisfy their curiosity? Let's say: the background, the usefulness, the motives, the results, when and where the idea had first come to him, the potential contribution of the discovery, in short —an explanation. What all the fuss was about. What the point of it was.

Pomeranz hesitated.

Then he softly agreed.

Almost at once he was seized by excitement. A thrill he had not known for a long time suddenly swept through him.

He cleared the table, smoothed out the cloth, and served coffee to his guests. As always, the room was filled with a faint, pervasive smell which was not the smell of the coffee or the smell of the flowers, perhaps not a smell at all but something which could not be put into words.

So they exchanged views on Syria, restraint or retaliation, and once again the conversation began to die down.

One of the two middle-aged women, a shrivelled but almost violently energetic woman, suddenly slammed her coffee cup down on the table and said :

'It's well known that great men are modest. Sometimes even shy. They need to be encouraged. Everybody needs to be encouraged.'

She cited the example of a celebrated violinist, Abrasha Auerbuch, who used to live in Czestochowa, and also that of Berl Katznelson, the Zionist leader. Boastfulness, she said, was always a symptom of insincerity. And things didn't always turn out for the best.

Her comrade, who worked in the sewing room, but also made ornamental ceramic animals, argued that it would be wrong to accept Vera's opinion without realizing that the matter was not so simple :

'But on the other hand, not everyone who is shy or modest is a great man. There are many shy people whose shyness hides nothing but a lack of self-confidence, as you, Vera, know better than most, and in fact you too, Ernst, and perhaps Elisha as well. Next Friday night, Elisha, we'll arrange a small party for you in the dining hall. Tamara will play something suitable on the piano, Ernst will say a few words of introduction, and then Elisha will explain to us once and for all what all the fuss it about. If you could hear what people are saying, what they're thinking, you'd be amazed, or even offended, but no, why offended, I'm sure it would make you laugh. At any rate, the upshot is that we also have a right to know something. At least to try to understand.'

'There are rumours.'

'Excitement.'

'Outsiders come and ask us questions and we shuffle our feet because we don't know what to say.'

'People say.'
'They guess.'
'They want to hear you.'
'Come out of hiding.'

Pomeranz put his hand over his mouth; perhaps he was feeling for his lost moustache. He nodded.

The faces of the two middle-aged women assumed an expression of pleased surprise, of a delight which was almost too sweet for them to bear.

Pomeranz vaguely remembered that one of the other shepherds had told him once about Ernst and his two mistresses, Ernst and his crazy son, Ernst and the wife of some British magistrate or administrator, the underground, and so on.

Ernst himself meanwhile weighed the whole conversation in his mind. The word 'hiding' which Sara had just uttered momentarily enchanted him. He emptied his pipe, taking care to put all the charred tobacco in the ashtray and not drop the slightest speck on the table, eyed his pipe for a while and then started to speak again. He drew his words out slowly and very purposefully.

There was always something peculiar about Ernst's manner of speaking, and on this occasion it was ever more marked than usual; he seemed to be subjecting each and every word to a slow, thorough examination before releasing it from his mouth.

He said:

'The news took us by surprise. We were not prepared. We learned it from the radio and the newspapers, without the slightest warning. Such things do not happen every day here. You must understand, Elisha, that it is not easy for us to find the right words to express exactly what is in our minds at the present juncture. We need to adjust gradually. We need more time. There are certain to be doubts and even suspicions. There will be some who will refuse to believe. Here and there there is bound to be a hint of jealousy, even of baseless and unfounded dislike. Even I myself am not yet certain what my thoughts and feelings are, because I do not understand what it is all about. I do not harbour suspicions, but I am still far from convinced. I am waiting. That is to say, I need more time. So much for my own personal position. Needless to say, our congratulations still stand. As for the kibbutz at large : no doubt there were some amongst us who were immediately carried away and already view themselves as partners, not to say relations. But so far as concerns the majority of the kibbutz, the average reaction, most of them, like me, still need more time. They need to adjust gradually. To draw the proper inferences. There have been disappointments in the past, left right and centre, disappointments, deceptions, disillusionment. We do not know you well, Elisha, we hardly know you at all; forgive me for speaking frankly. And it is not entirely your fault that we do not know you. There have been those who have taken an interest, wanted to help, tried to approach you. Everyone knows the facts : Elisha the shepherd, a solitary man, a survivor, an excellent worker, quiet, meticulous, prefers his solitude, mends watches. Yes. And gives math lessons. Doesn't talk. Cuts himself off, more or less, from the society of others and from communal responsibility. How should I put it to you; perhaps I should express it like this : Once or twice we have thought certain things about you. Our intentions were good. You know that. But who would have imagined that it could have come to this. You can easily understand that we are all proud of you and at the same time somewhat perplexed. Won't you give us a little more time. Well, it's getting dark. Thank you, Elisha, for the orange and the coffee and the cookies and what I regard as a frank and open conversation. If you need anything, you always know where you can find me.

Anything we can do for you we shall do willingly and
gladly. Now we must take our leave. Vera. Sara. Let's
go. Good night. Hugs are not my style, but you won't
get away without a handshake. Here. Congratulations.
Good night, and . . . good night, Elisha.'

25

The visitors departed. Outside, the lamps came on.
Inside the room there was a solemn stillness. After a
while Elisha Pomeranz, too, went out, to take a stroll
alone in the dark. It was Sabbath. The sound of record-
ers had die away. Now choirs of well-scrubbed children
sang Sabbath songs in the background. The sound was
high and pure. There was a bite in the winter air. In
the darkness to the east the shadow of the mountains
could be sensed. Mieczyslaw King of the New Poland
wore a greatcoat, and on his head a battered Jewish
cap. His stick in his hand. And the dog ran ahead of
him in the dark to lead the way. He was a stunted,
tawny creature, who had come from no man's land,
from the rocks, perhaps from the Syrian side of the
border. The hang of his tail suggested a touch of jackal
or a touch of fox. He held his nose out in front of
him till it almost touched the muddy ground and
panted, a sick yellow glint in his eye, his ears drooping,
his tail dangling limply between his legs. He always
looked as though he had just been beaten and was
plotting his revenge. And he was constantly seized by
fits of throaty hiccups.

Pomeranz closed his eyes. He walked slowly behind
the dog as though fighting against a strong headwind.
But the wind was not a headwind, it was a gentle breeze.
He probed the darkness with his stick, and detected a

thick, almost viscous quality in it. With his eyes still closed he saw the treetops, and mentally noted the sadness of the wind which was hopelessly entangled in them, and beyond the treetops, the counterfeit ocean depths of the stars. Hidden crickets sent signals in a strange language. A jackal started to wail and at once fell silent.

The Pole belched slightly, pawed the ground, leaned with his elbows on the music of the hills which streamed toward him from all sides. He was convulsed by the effort, his teeth were clenched, his shoulders strained. Eventually he managed to tear himself free and rise a few inches above the lawn, a short sharp hover, and at once his powers gave out and he sank to the ground.

The earth felt like velvet to him, and repentantly he breathed it, a warm, smouldering sound, a low hhhhhhh like the swish of the pines.

There was peace all around.

And in him.

26

Spring had come. The snow began to thaw, the birds returned from their wanderings, and in the suburbs of Moscow there were rowboats on the lakes once more. And Mikhail Andreitch, too, or whatever his name might be, returned from Palestine, laden with photographs and tape recordings and numerous stories, all of which he laid before the Chairman of the Sixth Bureau. As usual, he embellished his stories with skill and elegance, cheerfully exaggerating and lingering on trivial details to the point of exasperation. He spoke for three days and nights without stopping, except when ordered to serve tea; even when she dozed Stefa heard his voice, she strayed into dreams and still he did not stop talking.

He told with amazement of the beauty of the landscape, the energy of the Jews, the pitiful dimensions of the River Jordan, the building of the country by miscellaneous immigrants on principles beset with contradictions. He spoke too of the military, the economic, the scientific potential, and about the nature of the human material : mad Yiddish watch-menders who invented theorems and provided proofs, pallid Polish peddlers, and up in the hills of Galilee a simple shepherd of remarkable powers, who was either a charlatan or a genius. The photographs showed, the recordings were clear, perhaps somewhere far away in the hills the ultimate solution had been found. It may be, Comrade Fedoseyeva, it may be that we have certain possibilities open to us, startling possibilities, if it is not just a snare and a delusion. There may be hidden powers, revolutionary sources of energy. How can I, bumpkin that I am, comprehend such subtleties. This may lead to secret rays, absolute weapons. Surely we may be struck by total fear and panic, Comrade Fedoseyeva, at the unfolding of the mysteries of the universe. And from now on anything is possible, absolutely anything, I can't tell you, forgive me, I can't tell you how frightening it is. Just touch us with your fingertip, you will see that for some time we have been shaking, shaking with fear like a little child. Yes. I'll stop at once. Right away, Comrade Fedoseyeva, at once, immediately, you see, three four hush. Andreitch is quiet as can be. Distinctly silent.

At Easter, when she had a holiday, Stefa went to Novosibirsk for a few days as the guest of the Deputy Commissar for electrical engineering. This man, who was a great expert on the poetry of Pushkin and court scandals in pre-Revolutionary Petersburg, had been pursuing Fedoseyeva for some time and had even sent her an epic poem he had written. He was swarthy and heavy-featured, was missing his left arm, and had a colourful collection of military decorations. His name was Kumin, Engineer Kumin, and there were many who disliked his sharp mind and grim sobriety.

Kumin welcomed Stefa in a bearskin coat, and conveyed her by snow car to the temporary office which he had set up in a small hotel. After ceremoniously helping her off with her coat he helped her to two or three glasses of vodka and then immediately offered her a choice of programme : a meal, a rest, a conversation, or an outing, or any combination of some or all of these possibilities, in any order she chose. Stefa, coldly and politely, beguiled Kumin with one of her most direct smiles, till his chin shook and his flow of words stuttered to a halt. She would like to go out, provided that he himself would be her guide, and choose and explain what he considered to be the most interesting sights.

Did the Deputy Commissar really hope to deceive Stefa, to conceal his wild fantasies, as if he were not trembling all over like a powerful engine.

They went by snow car to inspect the project between the mountains and the lake. The dazzling whiteness of the snow forced them to put on dark glasses. Kumin laughed and exclaimed all the time, more like an enthusiastic schoolboy than a Deputy Commissar. And Stefa with her white hand offered him an occasional tiny glimmer.

They drew up alongside a row of monstrous transformers, and Kumin delivered a few casual explanations. His distraction was so evident that the men who accompanied them secretly sniggered. The sharp-sighted Commissar noticed and dismissed them with a wave. In the underground engine rooms they were escorted only by his most personal secretary and a senior technician. But not even these two were permitted to follow them into the office. At the door Kumin bowed, bumped his head on the doorpost, sprang back, half pushed his guest into the room and locked the door behind them. He stood facing her, looking woebegone and lost.

Suddenly he seized a stick and without a word began pointing to the plans and diagrams which lined two of the walls. Now, thought Stefa, he's going to turn the lights down and kneel in front of me, or lash out suddenly with the stick and hoist my dress over my face.

But Kumin neither knelt nor attacked her. Instead he collapsed into the armchair, covered his face with his one hand, and began to stammer that they were not really strangers, they were not just chance acquaintances thrown together by circumstances, no, they were brother and sister, and no power in the world could sever such a blood tie.

'I . . . I've no idea what you're talking about, Osip Grigorich.'

'You are my sister, Comrade Fedoseyeva, why do you mock me, why this game of hide-and-seek, you are my sister and I am your brother, and that's that.'

'Then I must be either drunk or mad, because I can't understand a word you're saying.'

'*Lehayim. Yom Kippur. Mazzeltov. Yisroel.* We're brother and sister, Comrade Fedoseyeva. Not two but one. *Yomtov, Boruch-Ato.* We two are one being, whose heart longs for its own land. You must surely have heard, in your work, how things are there, in our land, why are you silent, why don't we fall into each other's arms and weep hot tears together? There is no snow there, no wolves or bears, but there our Jews sow in sunshine, run, kiss, breathe in sunshine on our mountains and there they write poems or keep cats or plant avenues of trees there on our mountains, a Jewish mountain, Comrade Fedoseyeva, and it doesn't collapse, it stands solid and high, just a Jewish mountain, as if it was the simplest thing in the world to be a Jewish mountain or a Jewish sea or forest, or even just a plain Jewish log for all the world like any other damned log, a Bulgarian log, a Turkish log, only it's a Jewish log in a Jewish country. Can our tiny mind grasp it, Comrade Fedoseyeva? And what does it all amount to, apparently to a deep and terrible desire to live and to touch everything, even to trip over it, to stumble and fall, it means a peace treaty between Jews and the tanglible sphere, and for a given number of tangible objects within a limited territory a peace with Jews. With Jews, Fedoseyeva my dear, with Jews like you and me, come, cling to me, my sister, it means the conversion to Judaism of a strip of land, its water, its woods, its fields and plains, as if at long last some god has taken pity on us, and in a flash everything is changed from now on the galaxy is preparing to tolerate us, to put up with our appearance, to endure our tunes, our smells, our jokes, no longer to harass us continually, even if it is only in one tiny corner, at the ends of the earth, in Lilliput. Suddenly we have all been granted a pardon beyond all hope, we have finally been forgiven, and there are beautiful Jews there who are sometimes permitted to forget and only remember when they have a mind to. And to dwell in sunshine and be called by their own names all the days of their lives, plant and walk and shoot and spit as they wish, there you're crying with me, my sweetheart, you can't stop yourself, don't try to hide it, we'll cry together for two minutes and then we'll dry our eyes and go and look at the turbines and after the turbines we'll go straight back to the hotel to my room to my bed and if you refuse so help me I'll blot you off the face of the earth, my lovely sister. Now here we have three pumps, the biggest pumps in Russia, between the three of them they can drain the whole Baltic Sea down to the last drop in a hundred and ten days. I mean in theory, of course. Just imagine, my dearest. Everything I was saying was only for the purpose of illustration, and for the same purpose I'll tell you a little story. My father was a kind of Hebrew poet, a kind of madman, a Zionist, a stray lamb in the streets of Odessa. All his life he wrote poems about Mount Carmel and Mount Tabor and Mount Moriah, about the wailing wall in Jerusalem, about the desert and the holy tombs. So great was his yearning that he fell suddenly ill. It was a kind of gut rot. It was pretty foul. The poor devil suffered torture, and all his family suffered torture too with the symptoms. My father was in agony for seven years. And I, being an absolute bloody bastard, I couldn't stand the sight of his suffering and a few years ago I packed him off to Palestine before it was the death of him or he was the death of me. And do you know, Fedoseyeva my darling, what became of him there in the land of his dreams in the twilight of his life? The old man settled down, no doubt on one of the hills to which he had always lifted up his eyes, among his holy tombs, and there, in his long-dreamed-of Palestine, among the hills and tombs, there the old man goes on to his dying day writing heart-rending poems of longing for some other Palestine, the real one. All with perfect faith. All in Hebrew. And in Biblical language.'

27

On Saturday evening, as previously announced, after some appropriate introductory music, the radio devoted a special programme to Pomeranz's sensational discovery.

The interviewers began by tackling Ernst, the Secretary of the Kibbutz Council.

In carefully chosen and well-balanced phrases, as if he were a head of intelligence being cross-examined before a large audience, Ernst responded to the request to describe some aspects of kibbutz life in general and in detail. In his slow voice and in carefully selected words he enlarged on the place of a creative thinker within the framework of a collectivist society.

Abruptly the voice of a young broadcaster rang out, describing in lyrical, ecstatic tones the landscape of Upper Galilee, the trees and rocks, the kibbutz, the idyllic flocks of sheep on the beautiful hillside, the neighbouring houses, the house itself, its four walls taken together and separately, the furnishings of the room, the vase of flowers, and then again the earth and sky and the modest porch. Even the dog was not left out. Only for some reason he was promoted to the rank of a pedigreed Alsatian.

Next they dealt briefly with the national significance of the event, and invited a panel of distinguished scholars to discuss the subject of infinity : Ancient Greece, Atomists and Pythagoreans, Kant and infinity, infinity and Cantor. Neo-Kantianism, too, and the inevitable failure of Gavronski and Hermann Cohen. Bolzano's hopeless entanglement in irresoluble contradictions in his attempt to explain mathematical infinity. In contrast, the modesty and humility of Einstein's attitude to infinity. Potential and actual infinity. Dedekind and Pearce. Inescapable absurdity. The challenge to human understanding.

The mental limitations of mere flesh and blood.

The silent irony of secretive Nature.

An excellent lesson in humility.

The impossibility of understanding infinity, and the consequent impossibility of understanding death.

And the result—mysticism. Metaphysical yearnings.

The hope of miraculous enlightenment.

Of redemption.

Of illumination.

Next an acid, rasping scholar recommending caution : this discovery too might eventually come to be refuted, as a clever exercise in mathematical deception. And, incidentally, a mathematical infinity was not unclaimed territory. It had been delimited once and for all by the Formalist school of Hilbert and from another angle by the school of Whitehead and Russell. It would be better, said the strident scholar, not to celebrate before the event. Time would tell.

Rabbi Doctor Erich Vandenberg, for his part, took this opportunity to remind listeners that the mystical Jewish teachings of the Cabala mentioned several different kinds of infinity, such as the Enveloped Infinite, the Enveloping Infinite, and the Supernal Infinite. Science itself had come, as it were—belatedly, as always—to make its peace with Faith, and it was in this perhaps that the real importance of the discovery lay, as a first step toward Redemption.

The chairman wound up the discussion by stating that this was a happy day for science and especially for the Israeli scientific community, and above all else this was a unique and moving human document. As he stopped speaking, the radio put out a piece of electronic music, followed by a look at motoring conditions or the problems in the Customs Department.

That night in the port of Piraeus the water succeeded in undermining and destroying a fishing jetty made of rotten planks. The sea water seethed and bubbled saltily from its depths. The waves arched up and pounded rhythmically against the sea wall, mounting and lustily hammering blow after blow, soft and then hard, ruthlessly, relentlessly, again and again to the rhythm of its joy, sea within sea within sea. In the distance mountain peaks bit and tore at the crescent moon which they clasped in their jaws.

And a young woman stood all night at the window of her house facing the port in Piraeus, watching it all, and suddenly she dashed out of the house, never to return.

28

Meanwhile strangers continued to pour in : fortune seekers, the idly curious, all of them excited and enthusiastic. There were representatives, too, of foreign universities, research centres, celebrated scientific institutions.

Secretively, as though on tiptoe, emissaries also insinuated themselves from forces which preferred to remain in the background. Representatives of giant concerns and agencies cloaked in darkness. German-Belgian capital. A Swiss-American conglomerate. An Austrian agent representing a Progressive government. A black woman. A gang of young Latins in a car which looked like a pleasure cruiser. A pair of Greek Jews bearing a concrete proposal from the Far East.

Most of these visitors appeared to Pomeranz as astute, almost friendly figures, sharp-witted, at times as possessed of a cunning verging on virtuosity.

All of them, in their different ways and different languages, wanting to talk, to approach, to peer, to touch with their fingertips, to snatch a spark, however tiny, to take something at least away with them, to gain a glimmer of understanding, to make friends with the great man at all costs.

The members of the kibbutz, at least among themselves, called the visitors 'the Pilgrims.'

All of them without exception sniffed the theorem with dilated nostrils, groped for its ramifications, pursued the possibilities which might, who knew, result from just this new discovery :

Mysterious rays which could operate even at a great distance.

Accumulations of a new form of energy, wonderfully

simple yet amazingly potent.

The incidental conquest of some of the most powerful laws of nature.

An absolute weapon which nothing could withstand.

The vacuum.

The defiance of gravity.

Remote control.

A possible approach to the essence of the earth's equilibrium.

A check on the forces of the universe, or the ability to balance them one against the other as the need might arise.

Inconceivable powers whose possessor would have an unchallengeable domination which could not be undermined until Doomsday.

Total mastery.

Pomeranz, as though he felt his private life to be besieged by these fervent crowds of visitors, tried for a time to evade them. He asked the office not to pass on telephone messages, he did not answer letters. In the afternoons he hid in the library or the treasurer's office. Not here. Gone away. Busy. No visitors. No such person. Never was. Next month. Next year. That's flat.

But the efforts were all in vain. The more brazenly determined tracked him down even at the far end of the orchard, or discovered him in the evening sitting in the empty sewing room. So he abandoned subterfuge. He talked freely to them all, without distinction or discrimination, to groups and individuals, Japanese journalists or pure mathematicians from Glasgow, he described concisely and graphically the inherent power of music or the tranquillity of forests in autumn. His voice was relaxed and relaxing, almost didactic, trying to soothe each of them, to release them from the grip of inner claws. At times his face bore a hint of what appeared, to the more shortsighted, as well-mastered mockery. No doubt the thick jaws aroused suspicion. In his heart he was far from all taint of irony. In his own solitary way he felt almost sympathetic toward the wound of their burning desire to imbibe power. Japanese journalist, social reformer from Cornell, East European agent, team of Scandinavian cameramen, for an instant it became apparent that beneath their clothes their bodies were contorted by a terrible lust for the secret of power, for unimaginable variations on its delight, to dominate, to vanquish, to master, filled with a bitter, relentless yearning for omnipotence. This deformity, Pomeranz discovered, was more tormenting than carnal lust, more insidious than the lust for honour, stronger than thirst, depraving, corroding body and soul.

Every single one of them, young and old alike, Greeks, women, and Jews, all of them were in unceasing pursuit of the one thing Pomeranz might be able to give them.

In exchange for this thing they eagerly promised, with the merest of hints or the most disgusting of winks, to lavish on him:

Money.

Honours.

Women.

World fame.

All or any of these.

Elisha Pomeranz, tirelessly though with no great hopes, tried his best to set their haunted souls to rights. He gave them nothing, received nothing from them, he no longer tried to hide from them, he only longed to bring relief to his haunted haunters. To instil in them a different inner rhythm. To teach them rest. To wish peace to all men and to bring all men peace.

29

To wish all men peace and to bring peace to all men,
that was what Audrey longed for too. Along with five
or six young travellers like herself, Dutchmen, wrecks,
Americans, she had been living for some time on the
shore of the Red Sea, where summer never ends. There
on the beach they had built themselves a hut of broken
planks, and shared each other's dreams and daydreams.
They were bronzed by the sun, lean and bony, splashing and swimming in the sea, star-struck at night, slow
as though succumbing to gradual paralysis in this
dazzling region. Every evening the orphans sprawled
at the entrance to one of the hotels or night clubs, where
they played the guitar and sang soul-stirring songs,
holding out their hands for pennies. Mostly they waited,
even though for most of the time they did not feel, did
not know that they were waiting, waiting for what,
perhaps for a sudden voice from the wilderness, or for
the red mountains to move and mightily join in the
singing.

Meanwhile, it occurred to them to walk eastward some
time, to search out the soldiers guarding the Jordanian
border, and help them see the light.

One evening, when the fierceness of the sun was
somewhat assuaged, the barefoot orphans started walking
east along the shoreline. The smooth gravel scraped
the soles of their feet and added a sensual joy to the
spiritual joy which throbbed inside them. How enthusiastic they were, seeing themselves as poor apostles,
swept along by their mission, Jeff and Harry with
guitars and Sandy singing songs of peace, Audrey as
if windborne leading the way.

As the sun was being pierced by the mountain tips to

the west they reached the barbed wire, and there they halted.

The savage light had died, and now from the water there rose the water's gentle light. It was desert night; the sky turned to grey and the red mountains stood like the remains of a fearsome fire. By the barbed wire they found a small dugout, with sandbags and a casual trench, and outside the entrenchment on the beach Elyashar, Vilnay, and Adorno sitting peacefully smoking cigarettes. Like the newcomers the three soldiers were barefoot.

Jeff and Harry with guitars and Sandy singing songs of peace, and the soldiers quietly smoking and only half-turning to size them up indifferently. Then Vilnay stood up, cleared his throat, paused, suddenly pulled out a handkerchief and began noisily blowing his nose. Little Elyashar could not take his eyes off Audrey's body, but dared not look at her face. Adorno skimmed pebbles on the darkening water. And far away a hooting cargo boat. Doubtless manœuvring out of the harbour, doubtless lit up, doubtless heading for the Red Sea and the Horn of Africa, to the Indian Ocean and the Far East.

It was Adorno who spoke first, in crippled English: This is army place. No photograph here. What you want here?

These simple words raised shallow laughs on both sides. Did the travellers, could the travellers, have a camera? Then Sandy put his hand out, and Vilnay gave him a cigarette. And Jeff, who was a kind of spokesman, explained that killing only leads to more killing, but love begets love.

Within a few minutes the language barrier stifled the sermon.

Yet one word, one of his words, pierced the barrier and entered into their hearts, causing a certain change, a turn in the relations.

Elyashar, Moshe—a withdrawn boy from a religious

school—received and understood the English word 'love.' And he had never seen what girls have under their skirts, though twice he had sneaked into the cinema and witnessed a momentary flash of naked breasts. Now, as Jeff said the English word 'love,' Audrey stooped to get through the barbed wire so as to sit down with the soldiers. She was wearing only a length of cloth wrapped round her body, perhaps a coloured sheet, and as she bent down her breasts fell out and started to sway, and she pressed her arm against them, but they rebelled and a slight slap sounded, all in the grey light of evening.

Pain and humiliation suddenly got the better of Elyashar, Moshe. The bloodthirsty painted redskin stirred in his trousers, the tomahawk was brandished, and from all the caverns and hideouts came a war whoop of hatred and fury. Private Elyashar, Moshe began to gesture coarsely, snigger, and plead in guttural English; he even used bad language. An ugly gleam in his eyes and half his face twisted in a filthy smile.

Like a forest fire it seized hold of his comrades too. They trembled visibly. Suddenly a heavy bitter silence fell. The air grew dark. Not a sound was heard. The place was remote and far from help. Even the black water seemed to be seething and plotting.

The band of players turned to go. After a moment Sandy and Harry started running, dragging Audrey by her arms. She ran with them, tears trickling down her cheeks. Stones pursued them. Private Elyashar, maddened by his tortures, screamed outrageous curses after them in Arabic. Until the enemy soldiers beyond the border heard and cursed back with fourfold vigour.

Toward dawn light firing was heard. A complaint was lodged.

30

On the edge of the lake in the beautiful German town
of Baden-Baden stands a hut made to look like the
witch's house in *Hänsel and Gretel*. From this hut small
rowboats are rented for boating on the lake, mainly to
foreign tourists and nature-seeking couples.

One cold blue spring day the hut was being watched
from concealed vantage points by three strangers. All
three were young and athletic, with short-cropped fair
hair, strikingly good-looking and amazingly like one
another in appearance. They remained in their hiding-
places watching the hut.

One of them, hidden in the thick cover of an ancient
tree, was listening attentively to the earpiece of a tiny
wireless receiver. The second, concealed among the
reeds, kept the hut under constant observation through
the sights of an accurate, silent rifle. The third, wearing
a diving-suit, waited beneath the surface of the shallow
water for any event which might require his interven-
tion.

And now, down the path leading to the hut there
stepped a brisk little man, a short, small-fingered man
with batlike ears straining forward. He looked like a
rabbi who had turned his collar up as high as possible
and slunk out to an adulterous assignation on the edge
of town. He was not young, and the woman on account
of whom he had turned his coat collar up and dabbed
cologne behind his ears this morning, for whom he now
hired the best rowboat, alone with whom he gently
rowed into the centre of the lake—the woman was
not young, either.

But charming, and attractive, and exquisite in every
line.

She was tall and thin, with a gentle downward slope to her shoulders : she looked as though she had suddenly grown faint and needed support. This quality was deceptive, and even at a distance a second glance would reveal the ruthless strength contained in the line of her chin or the sudden movement of her small hand as it deftly brushed a speck of dust or a spot of mud from her green woollen dress.

Far out on the lake, as the clear blue sky shone down on Baden-Baden, Fedoseyeva suddenly donned one of her most precise smiles. The man was enchanted. He forgot his opening line, at once recovered himself. But Stefa anticipated him :

'It is a great pleasure for me finally to make your acquaintance after all these years. I am full of respect, full of admiration. Were it not that our profession deprives us of the right to compromising keepsakes I should ask you for your autograph here and now. What I mean to say is that I am one of your most devoted admirers. Now to come to the point. I cannot understand what your calculations show you. Which is your credit column and which is your debit column. I am making you a simple, straightforward offer : I am giving and it is up to you to take, with supreme caution. Why should you not take? I am not charging anything. And don't tell me you suspect a trick or a trap. Such a suspicion, as you must understand, greatly damages our mutual self-respect. Help yourself. I am all yours. Gratis and for nothing. Call it an emotional need. Call it a Zionistic impulse. I shan't change my mind and I shan't make any conditions, apart from the insistence that you receive me with enormous caution. But, after all, in the art of caution you are the great maestro. Let us decide on the necessary arrangements. Do not weary me with questions about the considerations and motives which make me suddenly choose to unbosom myself to a man like you. Then we'll say farewell and adieu. Do you accept or not?'

The little man did not answer at once. He mused for a while, and as he did so he closed one eye almost completely, as if to economize on his eyesight.

Suddenly he leapt up as if stung, almost upsetting the boat; quick as a flash he put his hand in his pocket and pulled out a lighter as Stefa fished her cigarettes out of her handbag.

Then he smiled, and when his companion did not smile back he closed his other eye too. And he started to speak, at length, with unfathomable patience and in a Talmudic sing-song:

'Yes, yes, Madame. Yes indeed. You can't have a baby through the mails, if you will forgive the expression. *Da,* I apologize, I apologize from the bottom of my heart for my choice of words. Excitement is my undoing, Madame. It was the excitement that made me adopt a vulgar and suspicious tone.

'I am sure you can understand my feelings, Madame. Here am I, here are you, there is no one else about, we are alone, floating on the water, and water—so I believe with all my heart—is a very important element, one of the mainstays of life. And so, Madame—permit me—Madame Pomeranz, so we meet in a strange town and row out to the middle of a lake in such extraordinary circumstances, and moreover we have, as you so rightly say, for many years had connections with one another, well, how should I put it, we have felt strongly drawn toward each other, we have spent long hours contemplating each other from a distance, there has been an emotional bond between us, and I am sure you will agree with me when I say that emotional bonds are the essence of the social structure. And what amusing games we have played with each other all these years. What naughty pranks we have got up to. I was about to compare our long-standing relationship to a flirtation conducted through intermediaries. But this time I held my tongue and said nothing. So, now we have met. It is still hard to believe. We were like dreamers, dear lady, if you will permit me to employ Biblical language. *Da,* language is an inestimable gift; who can exhaust its praises? But at once I pinch myself, Madame —so—and bang go all the excited dreams. Now, as you request, for the *realia.* I am wide awake and ready for anything. Command, Madame : the worm Jacob and the hind Israel hearken as one to the voice of Mother Russia. *Eh bien.* How blue the sky is; despite oneself one thinks of the poems of Goethe, or the visions of the romantic philosophers. And by the way, is Madame Fedoseyeva in earnest? Or does she mean to make fun of a lonely man who is no longer young, and make a laughing-stock of him—of me, that is—once and for all? Madame must try to understand me : I am a wounded man, I have already been badly hurt by young ladies – two or three of them. That was all a whole generation ago, however. Nevertheless, Madame, unworthy apprehensions, an incurable suspiciousness, a constitutional insecurity, a fear of the fair sex, certain prejudices—all these compel me to put your intentions to the test before giving free reign, as they say, to my emotions. I must have some token, some slight evidence of the seriousness of your intentions. For instance, a teeny-weeny droplet of the fuel which Engineer Kumin, Osip Grigorich, has been clever enough to manufacture. A tiny drop, enough perhaps to fill the lighter in my pocket, or else perhaps not a drop, no fuel at all, but the good Engineer himself might be induced to take advantage of this opportunity and join you on your journey. Moreover, when you come to us, as soon as the first joyful moments are over, I shall have to restrain our joy and connect certain plugs and disconnect others, to make certain alterations in the points of contact, a matter of elementary legerdemain whose purpose I shall not attempt for a moment to conceal from you, Madame : it is to block the escape routes, however fantastic they may seem. To burn all your bridges. And the purpose of this is to remove any feelings of regret, because regret is, in my humble opinion, a constant source of mental anguish. Let us give vent to words which our beloved Elisha Pomeranz would not use, but which we, being lovers of poetry, may legitimately employ : we shall remove you from the clutches of Mother Russia, and carefully and lovingly plant you, once and for all time, in the soil of Israel, in the hope and certain conviction that in the land of our fathers you will blossom and bloom sevenfold.'

Stefa :

'We understand each other, more or less. That is good. I must only repeat and emphasize that Palestine will have to take very good care of me and of him. My people will be furious, they have a long arm, the risk is grave. Incidentally, while you were mentioning Kumin and talking about solid fuel or something of the sort, songbirds began to sing among the trees and I could not hear that part of what you were saying. It is twenty past three.'

The little man :

'But of course, dear lady. Rest assured, as the apple of our eye we shall protect you, and the man who is so dear to you. With all due respect, between lovers such things should be understood even without words. We shall take perfectly good care of you both. Permit me, Madame, forgive me, I am a trite man and I am about to make a trite observation. To what end did we go through blood and fire to establish a free Jewish state? Why, first and foremost surely to provide a safe refuge for every persecuted Jew. And by the way, dear lady, surely you know something about us by now : we may bark at a shark—but we're kind to a hind. And here we have concrete illustration of the abstract idea of family reunion, of the notion of repentance . . . tears well up in our eyes, dear lady, and who would be fool enough to deny that tears are a sure sign of emotion?'

Fedoseyeva :

'Silence. Now listen with both ears. Any day between the second and the sixteenth of February, between six o'clock and ten o'clock in the evening, at the Albergo Ambassadore in Milan, have two women waiting for me. Women, not men. Two of them. And no one else. No hidden strangers, such as you saw fit to lay on for our meeting here today. A sign, by the way, of extraordinarily bad manners on your part. These two women who will wait for me, if they see me smoking a cigarette, they will know that I am not alone, that I have company. In that case they must run for their lives, because they will be in great danger. If I am not smoking when they see me, I am in their hands and everything will depend on their dexterity. Now we must part. Give no hint or clue for the time being to the man I am going to in Palestine. Only protect him from harm. If anything should happen to him, I shall be of no use to you and you will not see me alive again. Now make for the shore. Naturally you are free to tell me anything else if you so wish, I do not of course forbid you to speak to me, your manners are so evidently good, please say whatever you like. But you must forgive me if from now on I do not listen. Those birds are singing again. And I am suffering from migraine. Farewell. Remember to drive carefully.'

31

A week after Ernst and his two middle-aged lady friends visited Pomeranz's room, the following Friday night, the Cultural Committee planned a modest celebration of the discovery and its discoverer.

But an hour or two before the appointed time, the guest of honour suffered the loss of his dog. The dog had stretched his legs, stared for some minutes through the window toward the fading hills, or perhaps at the curtains moving in the breeze, then he had suddenly given way and died as if suddenly stricken with absent-mindedness or unbearable boredom.

They assumed that Pomeranz would be sad, and out of delicacy of feeling they decided to postpone the party. A dusty moon glowed in the east. And because there were no clouds racing across the sky, the moon stood stubbornly, solidly still.

In the dining hall they showed instead a detective thriller, a black-and-white American mystery about a crime, false motive, true motive. Pomeranz sat alone on the bench in the little garden opposite his house. Far away in the darkness a cow lowed stupidly, lowed again and stopped. Strange dogs, wolf dogs, stood huge and dark at the edge of the wood with wet snouts, raising their slavering muzzles to the moon. Through the pine trees a mad moon bit them. All night long the huge dogs howled.

32

Day by day Pomeranz's fame spread through the country and abroad. People with problems or aspirations continually wrote to him, came, probed. He pursued his nightly studies, making calculations by the light of his desk lamp, putting out cautious feelers in unimaginable regions where mathematics and music were as close as two separate rivers issuing from the melting of the same snows.

But what can simple folk know of the private life of the virtuoso, the daily routine of a man no longer young left alone with his body.

Prolonged celibacy: relations of pent-up boredom, of

faint disgust, with the inescapable body, with its whims, its demands, its impositions. For years he had found it repulsive. Its relentless, loathsome needs. There was no refuge from this blue-veined, capricious body, as if one were condemned to spending the rest of one's life shut up in a single room with some sweaty ageing relation, with swollen veins and foul breath. And endless grumbles and tantrums and denials and complaints.

The tightlipped effort to concentrate in spite of everything, to escape, to elude the foe, to explore and investigate a limpid, almost airless sphere, while all the time beyond the thin partition an excited girl laughs screams pleads as if she were being rolled in honey or having her soles pricked with tiny needles. Audrey Audrey.

Your body odour on the towel. Clench your teeth and restrain yourself.

The ruthless tyranny of the cheap alarm clock: Get up. Go to bed. Sit down.

The dishes in the sink.

The irritating tendency of the black shoe polish to dry and crack because the lid of the tin has not been put back quite straight.

The milk going sour too soon.

A dull, sticky taste in the throat.

Black coffee.

Heartburn.

A hacking cough in the early morning.

The stink of your ageing body which emanates even from the armchair, from the bedspread. The endlessly repeated sweeping. The invincible dust.

The daily carpet-beating.

And all the time the continual wheezing, like the wheezing of an old woman.

The humiliating need to remind yourself at such moments, you are the discoverer, you are the celebrity, you are the virtuoso, so pull yourself together and wash the dishes.

Talking to yourself—in Polish.

And the feeling of despair when you can't find a simple, everyday word.

The numerous petty irritations : a few grains of sugar fall on the floor, throngs of exultant ants appear, you snatch the insect spray and go out to do battle, at once a large paraffin stain starts spreading on your trousers.

Moments of carelessness : your sleeve knocks a cup off the table. It shatters on the floor. A pool of spilled coffee. And to drive the humiliating lesson home, the rug, too, is stained.

Or, say, the clean underwear finding its way by mistake into the dirty laundry, the teaspoon ending up somehow in your trouser pocket, comic mishaps, the laboriously replaced light bulb turning out to be a dead one itself, lemon squeezed into milk tea, all so shaming, and wasn't the whole point supposed to be the power to work wonders, to reveal something of the harmony of the spheres, to work some kind of salvation?

Over everything, like the glass eyes of a stuffed bear, this coarse bitter hunger, night and day, for a woman's gracious bounty.

Rise up and put off your flesh, and rest and peace will come. Could any truth be simpler than this.

33

When Stefa first visited Engineer Kumin in Novosibirsk he told her that his old father lived on top of a holy mountain in Palestine and wrote poems of yearning for Zion.

But Old Kumin merely lived in an old people's home in Givatayim.

In addition to the digestive disorder which had enabled

him to leave Russia, the old man also suffered from out-
bursts of melancholy and a dripping ear. He was a tall,
bent man of eighty-two, with rosy cheeks and cloudy
blue eyes. Despite his various aches and pains, there was
something strong and sharp about him, like a bird of
prey.

Even though he had never worn glasses and even now
his eyesight was adequate, his nose seemed somehow
bare and overprominent, as if he had just lost his spectacles and the outside world had become totally blurred.
He had a perpetual expression of dumbfounded malice.

Indeed, many people supposed him to be a foolish
old man. He was in the habit of appearing without
warning at meetings of poets, at conferences of educa-
tionalists and public leaders, pouncing on the micro-
phone with liberal use of his elbows and tongue, and
furiously denouncing someone or something in a strong
Russian accent and roars of rusty anger. He also penned
frequent letters to the editors of the newspapers vehe-
mently maintaining that this or that matter of public
interest was bound to end badly.

His deafness and his constant fury protected him
against every sign of disrespect or derision from the
ignorant masses. If they replied to his assertions, he
did not listen. If they argued with him, he did not hear.
Once during the Silver Jubilee celebrations Kumin
mounted the rostrum of the Trades Union Council,
stood over Prime Minister Eshkol, and loudly proclaimed: You, Sir, are a troubler of Israel. Before he
could be seized he had made with surprising speed for
the door and walked out of the hall in disgust. He returned at once to his room in the old people's home and
began composing a long and bitter epistle addressed to
the writer Haim Hazaz.

Before the Russian Revolution Gershon Kumin had
been a pharmacist, surgical assistant, and poet in Odessa.
In the course of his life he had suffered many colourful

vicissitudes, some of them noble, others base and degrading. Not only had he fallen in love as a young man with a non-Jewish girl student, but he was married against his will to a girl from the violently anti-Zionist Getzler family. When he sent some poems of yearning for Zion to the famous literary editor Ravnitsky, Ravnitsky wrote back that although they were priceless gems all the poems would need to be drastically shortened. And even though at the end of his letter Ravnitsky called him the 'sweet singer of Zion,' Kumin never forgot or forgave the abhorrent phrase 'drastically shortened.' Then the Revolution broke out. First his wife and then his only daughter fell in love with the bloody anarchist Fyodor Sosloparov and followed him to Samarkand, to the Chinese border, to Kamchatka, and there the three of them disappeared without trace. It was said that they had died, or committed suicide together, or that the steppe wolves had eaten them on their travels, or perhaps that they had managed to escape by boat to the Isles of Japan, or even to flee across the Bering Strait over the ice. There was a rumour at one time that the three revolutionaries had eventually reached Argentina, where they had made a fortune in canned beef.

Some years later Osip, the son of his old age, rose high in the ranks of the accursed Bolsheviks, and the turncoat sent his brother Mitya, who was an artist, to a labour camp in Siberia. Osip had perpetrated this outrage out of deliberate malice. For this deed the old man cursed his remaining child and said to him publicly on the Great Sabbath, The voice of your brother's blood cries against you, Cain, and he also said, Cursed and a servant of servants. He vowed that he would never see him again, and indeed he did not set eyes on him for nine years.

Only when Gershon Kumin succumbed to his unsavoury disease, and the authorities began to move him from place to place because of the complaints of all those around him, had Osip intervened and had the old man transferred from sanatorium to sanatorium, from one hell to another, until finally their mutual disgust burst all bounds. Then Osip signed a document which enabled the old man to leave Odessa for good and go to his ancestral land, which was not, by any manner of means, even the palest shadow of what it should have been. So that his heart wept and his soul pleaded at night to soar skyward and seek out the heavenly Jerusalem and the true Promised Land.

Small wonder, then, that when Old Kumin heard on the radio and also read reports in two newspapers about Pomeranz's discovery, he hastily sat down and composed a letter in which he posed a number of questions to the esteemed mathematician :

1. Was it true, as reported in the *Weekend Magazine,* that the whole universe was expanding? And if so, where was it expanding to and at the expense of what was it expanding?

2. The writer understood nothing of mathematics and did not give a fig for mathematics. The only significant question for him was the question of infinity, and that only with one end in view : was there or was there not an afterlife? Would he kindly answer yes or no, and if no, would he kindly admit that all the fuss was about nothing, infinity was no infinity and the discovery was no discovery.

3. If the whole universe was in fact subject to fixed laws, what room was there for the 'paradoxes' to which the article in the magazine referred? And if, notwithstanding, the discovery did involve 'paradoxes,' what authority was there for the arrogant assertion that the laws were in fact laws?

4. Why did scientists, even in the kibbutzim, shut themselves in ivory towers and preen themselves with all sorts of so-called 'universal' questions, instead of combating the decadence and degeneracy in the country and in the government?

5. How much longer?

It was nine o'clock in the morning when Gershon Kumin stuck a New Year's greeting stamp, and an 'express' sticker, and a 'registered' label, on his letter, and went out to mail it.

By three o'clock in the afternoon he was feeling impatient: would he get a reply, when would it come, would it be an adequate reply? His questions suddenly seemed to him of absolutely unsurpassable urgency. He had an attack of indigestion, to boot. So he got into his brown check suit, put on a tie, tucked a white handkerchief into his breast pocket. All without so much as a glance in the mirror. Then he snatched up his stick and hurried on his way, nodding his birdlike chin up and down all the while and muttering out loud, Yes, yes.

For five hours and fifty minutes the old man journeyed from bus to bus, from dusty bus station to dusty bus station, and in addition to the oppressive heat and the pain in his guts and his dripping ear he also began to be tormented by a feeling of furious self-hatred.

After sweeping northward through Samaria and the valleys like an evil spirit, he reached Galilee and alighted finally at Pomeranz's kibbutz. It was nine o'clock in the evening, and the old man was still as furious as when he had set out, if not more so. He immediately began to cross-examine two youths as to the whereabouts of the local sage and prophet. The stunned young men led him to Pomeranz's room. But at the very instant that Old Kumin's blurred gaze fixed on the square of light at the window, he suddenly underwent a change of heart. He was assailed by powerful misgivings. He may have recalled Tchernikhovsky's famous poem about the visions of the false prophets, or the contempt that the other great poet, Bialik, had heaped on the scoffers. In short, Kumin was filled with a terrible anger at himself, his letter, his stupid journey, revolutions, science, and youth in general.

Without a second thought he turned and strode through the night to the kibbutz gate. Somebody addressed him, inquired, spoke kindly to him, but he as usual did not hear, did not listen, took no notice. He found the winding road, and made his way back to the highway.

It was night. From the valley rose the snicker of frogs. The stars of Galilee shimmered. The gentle breeze seemed to sweep a delicate, stirring veil of light in its train.

The mountain air worked wonders for the old man. Suddenly he felt his lungs swell. An old song stirred in his heart. His journey was unexpectedly shortened: an army transport picked him up at the bus stop and whisked him quick as lightning southward, went out of its way for him and deposited him reverently outside the old people's home.

It was midnight when he went to bed. At two o'clock he was awakened by a vision of Galilee, the smells, the breeze, the wavering light.

Kumin lit his lamp and sat for two or three hours composing his famous poem 'The Soul of the Hills,' which has since been included in several school textbooks.

After he had written the poem Gershon Kumin's mind was at rest, his fury abated, even his digestive trouble improved somewhat, and, what was more, the dripping in his ear vanished without a trace. He had always detested miracles and suchlike, but on this occasion he permitted himself—after a serious inner debate—to employ for once the term 'grace.'

A week later he received a letter from his disinherited son Osip. As usual, he tore it up without opening it, without looking at it, without even sparing the rare stamps, and flushed the pieces down the lavatory. But for once he felt a pang of remorse deep inside him: was he not a mean, selfish, insensitive old man, what moral right had he to explode, to cause offence and sorrow, to cast doubt on a brilliant discovery, and even suddenly to call Prime Minister Eshkol 'troubler of Israel'?

He had a moral obligation to apologize at once. In writing.

34

Night in the beautiful German town of Baden-Baden.

The Dominican friary is surrounded by large walls and darkness. The chapel is deserted. Flagstones, wooden benches, high vaulting, biting cold. The organ is ringed with shadow. There is a slight restlessness in the air of the empty chapel. For several hours there has been no one here, no music, yet still something clings to the crannies in the walls. Majestic music has throbbed here, billows of melancholy grandeur, and now the ancient walls release it all like an invisible radiation. Four or five hours after the end of the Office, empty ancient chapels have a way of animating their darkness with vague stirrings. If the chapel is closed and not a candle is alight, and the thunder of the organ's yearning for celestial purity is broken up into distinct echoes, sound and silence, no-sound and silence, at such times the chapel should be left to itself. : Not be disturbed.

A single candle burns in a cell in a wing of the friary. A man of middle years, broad of body and large of limb, stands at the small barred window of his cell and stares at the moon, or perhaps at the shadows of the lonely poplar trees outside shaking in the wind.

In his left hand he holds a large, heavy razor. A single candle glows on the chest of drawers behind him. Because of the candle the steel of the razor gives off sharp flickers of light. At times it flashes with a red fire.

Deep in the outer darkness the friar can hear the roar of a night train, and the sudden wailing of the engine as it approaches a junction.

Through the bars of the window the man watches two lean girl students at the corner of the lane, beneath a yellow street lamp, writing, no doubt in red, on a dark wall. Presumably they are writing a slogan against the established order.

From the darkness of his tiny cell in the Dominican friary the lone watcher fancies he observes that the two girls are freezing in the bitter cold and one of them is even sobbing or perhaps rather chuckling in silent malice. The steel razor shoots a lightning spark into his watching eye, the white of the eye glows red, and now the friar too chuckles to himself and quietly grinds his teeth.

Then he puts the flaming razor to his throat. With his free hand he pulls his left ear. The back of his hand is extraordinarily hairy, a monkey's paw, and beneath the tangled black tufts the luxuriant flesh is as red as raw steak, as if there were no skin covering it. Thick dark-blue veins intertwine, seemingly unable to contain the throbbing of the heavy blood. Each heartbeat makes the blood vessels shudder and jump as if they are about to burst. Something is pushing, something is evidently struggling to burst out, a blind swell thrusting outward. This powerful body, there is no mistaking it, would never collapse under the weight of years or fade away in weakness; it would burst outward from the force of the pent-up tide.

Every morning, an hour and a half before sunrise, the big-boned friar is in the habit of shaving with a cut-throat razor and ice-cold water. He shaves at the window of his cell, without a looking-glass, from memory; he knows all the features of his face by heart, like a simple tune.

The breadth and coarseness of the jaws.

The heaviness of the chin.

The almost monumental span of the nostrils, like mighty, shameless arches.

The friar has also forsworn lather forever : nothing but blade and bare skin.

And so, with dry gleaming razor on dry cardboard skin, he cuts through the bristles with short powerful strokes like a lumberjack felling a forest.

Here is no self-mortification, certainly no joy of self-denial or humiliation of the flesh through pain, but, rather, the very opposite of all these virtues : his violent nightly shave affords him shudders of pleasure, a sensual enjoyment which he is neither willing nor able to conceal. He draws the finely stropped razor across his large jowl with strong, controlled strokes. He shaves cautiously at the point where the veins pulse warm and close beneath the skin, in the pit of the throat. The crackling sound of the bristles as they respond to the razor sends a delicious shudder down his back, fully arousing the big-boned body, spreading a flood of inner moans to the very tips of his toes, in his loins an exultant diapason, accompanied by tortures of boiling oil, of burning poison, flashes of criss-crossing sensations. Fire within ice.

All this takes place without the slightest haste. As slowly as the flesh can stand, luxuriously, drawing out every movement, savouring the echo responding from the depths, with great precision, with practised concentration and the utmost sensitivity.

And yet on closer inspection there is no doubt that this is all a constant striving toward spiritual ecstasy :

The very razor, a heavy, solid instrument when viewed normally, tapers gradually before your very eyes to a thin fine point, straining at its tip to rise upward, to escape from the realm of the physical. Just like a Gothic spire the razor is nothing less than solid matter straining on tiptoe toward distant ethereal heights, the gradual purification of steel whose very soul yearns ardently for insubstantiality, and more, to become pure idea or spirit.

And similarly the urgency of the blood struggling to burst out of the imprisonment of the flesh, to be released and become an unrestrained, unbounded flow.

And similarly the movement of the furry hand holding the razor with the precise grip of a virtuoso, as if there were no razor, no nocturnal shaving, but as if he were playing the violin to himself in his cell by candlelight, the Dominican Friar Topf.

And similarly the crackling of the bristles, a subtle variation on the crackling of mighty forests in a terrible summer fire.

And similarly the sensual pleasure streaming inward and assailing some crucial point in the pit of the stomach or at the base of the spine until the throat holds back a low groan and every nerve bursts into a rhythmic spasm.

And similarly with the first hints of murky daylight, the last rays of moonlight on the row of poplars in the lane. The friary walls. The two girls, too, laughing and freezing outside, or perhaps waiting for a sign. And the wailing of the train to the night's embrace. And the night itself, gradually dying away. The bars in the window. The crucifix on the cell wall. The pious books. The shame. The ecstasy. The creeping on of death. The smell of distant darkness. Suffering. Silence. Stony tranquillity.

35

The beautiful German town of Baden-Baden has been chosen as the venue for a world congress of mathematical logicians and philosophers.

The aged philosopher Martin Heidegger, despite being a rather controversial personality, is to deliver the opening address.

And now, at noontide, the red van of the Mobile Mail hurries up along the steep winding road among the gloomy Galilean hills. A cloud of dust surrounds the van, its horn blares, and Elisha Pomeranz too has received—in a large pile of otherwise uninteresting mail—an official invitation heavily embossed and sealed with a gold seal : the pleasure of his highly esteemed presence is requested and he is invited to honour the Congress by delivering a lecture on the subject of mathematical infinity. It is further requested that he be so kind as to submit in advance a synopsis or abstract of the lecture he proposes to deliver, for purposes of prior consideration and for the information of the other honoured participants. In expectant anticipation, faithfully and with deep admiration, Germany, such-and-such a date, such-and-such a year.

For several days Pomeranz weighed the invitation in his mind. He measured various angles and ranges, compared possible trajectories, as if he had been given the responsibility of digging a canal to link the new kingdom of Poland in the Isles of Greece with the Baltic—or else to dismiss the responsibility out of hand.

Suddenly he made up his mind to accept and to attend.

Mieczyslaw the First or Przywolski the Last, can it be that the powers will abandon you in the place where sentence will publicly be pronounced.

And if the powers do abandon you precisely at that time and in that place, even that can only be to the good.

Let it be the lion's mouth, the crowds of doubters and mockers, the place of bloodshed.

His decision filled him with excitement, almost with joy. He said to himself :

'So far.'

And also :

'The glass eyes of the stuffed bear.'

And :

'Heidegger in person. Heidegger himself.'

The Kibbutz Committee approved the journey at once gladly and in a friendly spirit.

At the same meeting they noted that Pomeranz intended to continue to devote half his time to the sheep, and that he intended to carry on as usual repairing members' watches and giving extra tuition to the backward pupils.

These facts created a positive and highly sympathetic impression. There were some who revised their previous bad opinions of Elisha. There were others who shrugged their shoulders and said, Well. Or, Very well. And, of course, there were others again who had their own ideas, who saw in all this devotion a pose of false humility which they considered worse than any pride or arrogance. Oh, look, he's taking his turn at dish washing in the dining hall, just like a mere mortal, just like one of us, quick, get a camera, you must get a shot of this, he's acting at being human, the Lord of the Infinite playing the Good Samaritan.

Moreover : It had become known from the newspapers that the new discovery had found many challengers. Doubts had been raised in several famous universities. A rash of second thoughts. Here and there also a letter or note in a learned journal. An Italian-Jewish professor who directed several research institutes on the west coast of the United States accused Pomeranz of fraud, of mathematical acrobatics; he asserted publicly that no solution had been found, that the equation was merely a desperately clever piece of hocus-pocus in the no man's land between the two main schools of logic.

On the other hand, an obstinate little teacher from Rotterdam emerged with the vague claim that he himself had already resolved the same mathematical paradox in 1939 and it was only due to his bad luck that the discovery had not been made public. In his address to the Soviet Academy of Sciences the Deputy Commissar for Science and Energy, Osip Grigorich Kumin, attacked the barren sophistry of certain futile theories being propounded in the West and their ramifications in Tel-Aviv. The speaker attached to all this sophistry the epithet 'talmudistic.'

Among the members of the kibbutz there were some who collected and circulated any such statement which appeared in the newspapers, even if only in the curiosity columns. Certain members derived pleasure from these challenges. They whispered and sniggered in private, revelled in rumours, and secretly awaited calamity. The collapse of the theorem. A minor, but colourful and heart-warming, scandal.

Most of the kibbutz members maintained an impartial attitude. How could simple folk be qualified to judge. It might be, or it might not. Wait and see. What are we expected to do. Certainly not to take any difficult decisions. There's no hurry : we'll cross our bridges when we come to them. There may not be any bridges to cross.

Meanwhile the backward pupils continued to come, dense but determined. To sit. To sweat. To belch. To strain their minds to the utmost. If they had a flash of illumination, their eyes lit up and they looked at him with inspiration. If there was no illumination they went home quietly, only to come back and try again in another day or two. Yotam, Ernst's crazy son, attached himself to Pomeranz and talked to him compulsively. But then, who had not fallen victim to the body's insatiable appetite for talking. He even used to speak to the doves, and lectured the oleander bushes, not to mention the girls, who were all forced to run away and hide when they saw him approaching.

The mothers of these girls would watch Elisha Pomeranz from where they sat on benches or on deck chairs in the cool of the evening, and say to one another :

'Fame and publicity are quick to come and quick to go.'

'We've seen all sorts of shooting stars in the past—and who remembers them now.'

'We had a lecture once about a piece by Borokhov which was very much to the point. It was called 'Castles in the Air.' Or maybe it was by Tabenkin.'

'It's like the fashions. Somebody turns up, creates a stir, and then disappears. That's the way it is.'

And they said :

'The whole thing's unreasonable. It's not natural.'

And they also said :

'Maybe *die ganze zach is a drey, a speculatsie, a gigantishe bloff.*'

36

The subject is the terrifying ruthlessness and desperate cunning of agents of various secret services. The story unfolds against a background of narrow alleys, deserted railway stations, and hotel lobbies in such towns as Milan, Turin, Locarno. The central character : an important figure in the Russian intelligence service, a woman, beautiful, extravagant, mysterious, who has decided to desert into the arms of the Israeli secret service, at great personal risk, because in the depths of her heart an ancient love has suddenly begun to stir, and for other reasons that are only hinted at. The night of terror is filmed in grey-black tones in sharp, nervous contrasts, while the memories of the central character, which are interwoven with the fast-moving action, appear in soft greys and reds, slightly hazy, like an impressionist painting. The dialogues are few and pointed. Most of the scenes are shot against a background noise of dimly throbbing engines. There is no music. Few effects. The atmosphere is one of silent, vicious violence, like a fight with daggers underwater. Milan. Night. Neon. A telephone booth. A Mongolian character, an expression of cruel cunning and ruthless stupidity, close-up, flat-headed Andreitch waiting in the darkness between two huge trucks parked in a side street. Cut. Hotel lobby. Waiters. A sheik wearing desert robes and gold rings. An old man in a wheelchair. Monkeys and parrots. Ice-cold beauties. A shortsighted man pushes between two gentlemen. A figure in a bridal veil. And in a flash two fat men firing after a speeding car, missing, firing again. They are shot from behind, they are not greatly disturbed, they operate some kind of flashing ray device, they are hit again, again they take no notice, they complete an electrical circuit, then they collapse in each other's arms like ballet dancers and suddenly they are both nothing but rag dolls filled with synthetic stuffing. Then a change of colour. A change of rhythm. A background. A distant view. And once more grey-black, night, sharp cuts. A freight plunges into a ravine. A light aircraft lands without lights and in an instant takes off again and proceeds on its way. It is night, someone is a hair's breadth faster than the rest, someone causes a clever diversion, someone is caught in a trap and gnashes his teeth, a flashing movement in the gloom, a shadow changes shape, there is a betrayal, a coup, fury, then the night pales and stillness settles over all. The production benefited from the support of the Cabinet minister who came from the same town as Stefa and Pomeranz and had once belonged to the Goethe Society. The man who looked like an adulterous rabbi returned to his shabby bachelor apartment on the outskirts of Old Bat-Yam and slept alone there for two nights and a day, then extended his short triumphal holiday by a day and advanced two pages in his private researches into the unexplored origins of the bitter rift between the rival talmudists Eibeschutz and Emden in the eighteenth century, and here too he made discoveries which no previous research had brought to light. As for flat-skulled Mikhail Andreitch, he was not slow to grasp the consequences of his failure and sought political asylum in America. After rendering some assistance and receiving his reward, he earned his living for a time by playing the part of old-fashioned Russian landlords in films, also specializing in unscrupulous villains and aristocratic émigrés. Eventually he landed in Argentina, where, if there is anything in the rumours, he made a fortune in the canned-beef trade.

37

Meanwhile, Galilee woke up to the billowing perfumes of spring. Each morning everything was bathed in moist sunlight. Brooding hills suddenly burst into ecstasy, blazed with red anemones, whirled heedlessly, dizzy in the ever-changing light. And close up : Some butterflies. The drone of a bee. The low buzz of flying ants. Dewdrops at dawn. New birds with new songs. And the buds appeared.

Elisha Pomeranz too appeared each morning on his way past the kibbutz office, a dwarfish figure in working clothes, his hat uncompromisingly hiding the upper half of his head, a shepherd's stick in his hand. Through the office window Ernst, unseen, suppresses a smile and raises an eyebrow : Really? And at once he returns to his work at the duplicating machine : Really.

Each morning, three or four days a week, Pomeranz tended the sheep. Each evening he sat in his room. If he had a visitor he offered him coffee and cookies. Ernst's two middle-aged lady friends, Vera and Sara, made themselves responsible for seeing to it that he was never short of cookies. Sometimes there were other volunteers. He carried on a light, intelligent conversation with his guest : music, the hopes for progress and its dangers, things in general, things here and now. Occasionally the guest would start talking about emotional stress; he might given an example from his own immediate experience. Elisha would listen attentively, would sometimes answer gently, and even hint vaguely at a tranquillity, at a possibility of peace even when it seemed there was no peace to be had. Then he would stop talking and give his undivided attention to whatever was said, even if it was very dull.

He also listened constantly to other sounds, such as the rebellious throbbing of the water in the water pipes, the shriek of a child on a distant lawn, the seduction of passing breezes and the pine trees' response, the starlight at night, the simmering of wind-struck fields, the whisper of silence just before the dawn.

His room was always as tidy as he could keep it, a place for everything and everything in its place. Almost as if it were uninhabited. And there was a faint, disturbing smell, perhaps somewhat sour, perhaps not a smell at all, an elusive presence, the imprint of a fussy bachelor who senses the approach of old age. It caused at times a moment's irritation, since the man could not accustom himself to this new element, or resign himself to it.

He rendered unto the kibbutz what belonged to the kibbutz, and when his work was done he shut himself up in his room.

Modest but meticulous principles governed the ordering of his day. Rising early he did six or seven vigorous exercises of Indian origin which Professor Zaicek had disseminated among his friends and acquaintances thirty years previously in the town of M——. The Professor himself, however, had never practised them, for they were far beyond his physical powers.

After the exercises Elisha went outside in his working clothes, which gave him an unbelievably clownlike appearance. So dressed he passed the window of Ernst's office and entered the dining hall. A thick doorstep of bread. Marmalade. Olives. Greasy coffee. From there to the sheep pens and from there with his flocks to the pastures.

By six o'clock in the morning the early spring light has spread over the plains. Sadness sounds from the hills. The wind of passing time blows faint and deadly. Across the valley the farmyard can be seen wrapped in a light morning mist. Large shapes slowly rusting in the scrap yard, around all the farmyard, coils of barbed wire, up which wild plants climb and twine in an effort to assuage their ugliness. Wooden towers fitted with searchlights stand at regular intervals along the fence. Each tower rises out of the barbed wire as if it alone existed, and there were, there could be, no other searchlight than its own.

Around the corrugated-iron sheds the agricultural machines stand swathed in silence, wrapped in oiled sackcloth, as if they were Russian bears transported to these sun-smitten regions, and now lying panic-sticken and motionless.

At lunchtime in the dining hall, meatballs with potatoes, mostly garnished with fried onion. Girls. Notices. Letters and mimeographed news-sheets. Fruit compote for dessert. Handsome young men in blue overalls. Old men with faces carved from gnarled wood. Elderly thin-lipped women who a generation and a half before had suddenly declared war on Nature itself. Now the fight was still not won, the elderly women were still here, still uncompromising, still on guard.

Somewhat apart several bald or white-haired men of ideas huddled round a table. They were forever deep in arguments about an article in the newspaper, an event, deviation, the sudden and unnecessary death of one of the founders of the Cooperative or the Farmers' Union, political events, what's happening, why, where will it lead, what's the lesson, what's the hidden meaning of the general situation.

From the kitchen wafts the rich smell of baking pies. And sauerkraut. The debaters offer no comment.

After lunch Elisha Pomeranz would take a stroll along the shady paths. He walked slowly, with his stick, a spiritual gait, those who saw him said, a *continental* way of walking. As if he were deep in convoluted calculations.

And waiting.

After his stroll he would devote some time to his garden : weeding, pruning, hoeing, watering a little. It was a miniature garden, laid out on a meticulous plan : four or five kinds of cactus were planted in crevices in some rocks, which were arranged in two symmetrical semicircles, prevented from meeting by two identical shrubs trimmed as neatly as sentries.

After his gardening comes the moment for a short afternoon nap. Even in his sleep a kind of calculation sometimes takes place, a process of equation. An unstable equilibrium.

At the end of sleep the world is dark. The walls of the room are black. The rectangle of the window is still grey.

Coffee. Cookies. A cigarette. Wash the cup. Dry it and put it back in its proper place. Wipe the table. Slight hesitation, what else to do with the cloth. Decision : dust the windowsill. Shake out the cloth. Change the water in the vase—on second thoughts, change the flowers as well.

The evening newspaper. Israel has once again warned; her enemies once more threaten. Commentary. Counter-commentary. Oddities and Anecdotes. On the inside pages : Speeches. Natural disasters. Development programmes. The renewal of an old public controversy. And now, time for the radio, the news, and the daily review. Perhaps, too, a brief musical interlude. Everything is obliterated by the smell of the evening, which is a gentle, poignant smell here. A few powerful longings pierce the soul to its depths, until the desire to die now to die this evening to die like suddenly shattering at a blow some tormenting blinding searchlight becomes overwhelming. Consideration of possible means. A fleeting memory insinuates itself and is repelled at once. The final possibility, if not to die at this very moment, to devote oneself to mathematical speculation.

And the evening itself : The yellow electric light. A change in the appearance of all the inanimate objects in the room. Once there was a dog, admittedly a wretched dog, a questionable dog, an impossible dog, but now there is nothing and the shadow of the bookshelves changes or moves without the shelves changing or moving, and what can help or sustain you at this moment.

Beyond the window the night blows invisibly. The hills

of Galilee, grey boulders and a solitary olive tree on the slope. To the west the black wind. There is no peace for the darkened valleys, something is rising up in the night, something is mounting, gathering, something is silently happening. What is it, what does it intend to smash and shatter? Who is behind it?

The man standing alone at the window of his room in the kibbutz in the hills of Galilee senses and knows facing him in the living darkness only hills upon un-peopled hills which pretend to be hills but are not hills but abstract longing which has taken on for a while a covering of stones and cypresses. For the time being.

A few minutes after eight o'clock his pupils start to arrive. They come into his room hesitantly, almost timidly, tapping lightly on his door, entering, taking two steps inside and then halting confusedly as if they prefer to leave him the option of changing his mind and throwing them out into the night. They sit, un-believably, on the edge of their chairs. Their shrinking timidity is all the more amazing because the boys are overgrown young men with large hands, with black grease hardened under their fingernails, with broad coarse foreheads and powerful shoulders, and the girls too are ample and powerfully built. Yet, as they process into Pomeranz's room, something makes them step delicately, as if they were tight-rope-walking. And they arrive punctually at the time arranged. They sit and learn to solve simple equations and to prove theorems in geometry. Restless, confused, trapped wild animals. Only one of them comes not to learn but to pour out ideas to Pomeranz; that is Ernst's son Yotam. He is happy to stand talking for a long time at the door, or simply to doze in the only armchair in a corner of the room while the radio plays classical music and a back-ward pupil has a lesson. Pomeranz has the pupil sit down at the table, gives him a glass of lemonade (ignoring a muttered refusal), and now he plots a few simple curves for him on graph paper, solves some equations in one unknown, constructs triangles with the help of a fork and two cake knives, draws tangents, compares various magnitudes in his examples. Yotam, if he is present in the room, takes no part and seems not to hear.

On occasion one of the pupils receives illumination. He stares at the page and the equations with wide-gaping eyes and mutters over and over again : I see, yes, now I see.

When the private lessons are finished, a little after ten o'clock, he takes up his stick again and goes out for his evening walk. Squares of light in the windows of the veterans' quarters. The sound of the radio. Sounds of laughter. A woman grumbles in Yiddish.

For a while he paces the paths by lamplight, then goes down to the end of the avenue, recalling perhaps for an instant the image of Jaroslaw Avenue. He smokes a last cigarette in the dark. His face is clouded. The night hurls night sounds at him. The King of Poland in the Isles of Greece sinks slowly into his night silence. Then he returns to his room. He fiddles with the radio and finds a distant, European station, which plays late-night music. He sits at his desk and gives himself over for twenty or twenty-five minutes to his equations.

And suddenly, enough.

He gathers up his papers. Puts them away in the desk drawer and locks it. Hides the key in the hem of the curtain. Absently turns off the radio. And prepares his body for sleep. If some small hindrance occurs at this stage, if the tube of toothpaste splits open at the bottom or his pyjama cord gets tangled in an obstinate knot, he says a couple of sentences to himself in Polish. Then he turns out the light at the head of his bed.

Slumber :

Howling wolves. Vampires. Axe blow. Forests upon forests. Snow. Greek music. American banknotes. Audrey. That is: simple elements and violent combinations.

And once more before dawn the blaze of sunrise casts a spell on the eastern mountains as if a mournful orgy is coming to an end somewhere just at this moment, gradually fading away in the distance beyond the rugged eastern skyline.

Sometimes the shepherd and his flock are joined by two large Alsatian dogs which belong to young Shaulik, the son of Yehuda Yatom. Shaulik is responsible for the sheep.

Lost in their dreams the sheep scattered on the hillside lazily crop the grass. At times they stop and stand motionless for a long while staring toward the Galilean hill light at the sky's edge.

And then suddenly one of the sheep raises a startled head and lets out a long, bitter bleat from deep inside her, as if in response to a sudden faraway call.

At the same instant the two Alsatians also bristle with a vague dread, a fearful growl rumbles deep in both their throats, turns hoarse, wails as if suffocated underwater, and expires.

And down they both sprawl once more in repose.

38

The philosopher Martin Heidegger tried to see in the fear of cessation and the constant presence of death a new key to the understanding of the riddle of the connection between Time, Being, and Thought.

In his celebrated work *An Introduction to Metaphysics* (1953), he is repeatedly at pains to explain that the German word *ist* is a word possessed of different and even contradictory meanings. In illustration of this he quotes a charming collection of random sentences in each of which the word appears 'in a use which is so common that we scarcely notice it. We say: "God is," "the earth is," "the lecture is in the auditorium," "the man is a Swabian," "the cup is made of silver," "the peasant is out in the fields," "the book is my property." '

And a little later:

' "The enemy is in retreat," "there is famine in Russia," "the dog is in the garden," ' and so on.

Finally Heidegger cites a pair of famous lines from a poem by Goethe:

Uber allen Gipfeln
ist Ruh,

which may be translated:

Over all hilltops
is rest.

From all these examples Heidegger draws support for the conclusion at which he arrives, apparently, with extreme reluctance: language, by its very nature, is always misleading. And particularly so in those matters which are the foundation of our existence. Hence it is our duty to purify and refine our language, to create a proper language, before we weigh anchor and set sail for unknown worlds, for the secret realms of Time and Being.

Indeed, from the time that the University of Freiburg was purged of Jews and Professor Heidegger was appointed its Rector with the approval of the Nazi authorities (1933), the philosopher did not cease to seek a possible loophole that would allow the crust of the deceptive language and conventions of thought fossilized in distorted grammatical structures to be pierced. Tire-

lessly and assiduously he strove to penetrate to the
sphere of mystery, to the depths of the secrets of Being.
He attempted to touch the enigma with fingers of
Reason, with an ascetic refusal to employ words or
forms of speech that had not been tested in its light. But,
to his great embarrassment and perplexity, in the middle
'forties the régime in Germany suddenly changed,
foreign ideas were carried into Germany on foreign
bayonets, and the old philosopher was involved for a
time in misunderstandings and unpleasantness.

So a man assails words with all the spiritual power
at his command, he struggles to capture in words the
existential dread, so he lifts up his eyes to the restful
hills, and suddenly the ground changes underneath his
feet : the enemy is in retreat, there is famine in Russia,
the dog is in the garden, and he himself is suddenly
sinking in pork fat.

39

Ernst, the Secretary of the Kibbutz, thought to himself :
It may be that we have a real mathematical genius
living with us here. But in fact he is not living among
us. He takes no part in the general assemblies, he con-
tributes nothing to the committees, he takes no interest
in the great questions like the reform of society or the
future of the Movement and the State, and even the
small questions on which our daily life is built do not
concern him. On the other hand, he does mend watches.
He helps the backward school children. He takes
the flocks to pasture. This is all well and good, but
it will lead to no good.

Each detail must be closely examined in turn. Examined under a bright light, to see the tiny blemishes, to
see where precisely the trouble starts.

The matter of the watches: no complaint. Excellent workmanship, and a laudable social gesture: even though you all know and none of you can forget for a moment who and what I am, yet I am not proud, success has not gone to my head, bring me your watches and I shall be, for two or three hours each week, your humble servant.

The case of the private lessons is more ambiguous. In some instances the man has worked wonders in setting boys and girls on the right track and instilling in them a deeply rooted respect for law and responsibility and for learning in general. Very good. On the other hand, there is something about him which upsets their calm and peace of mind. He arouses in these young adolescents, especially the girls, all sorts of undesirable reactions and undefined emotional disturbances: they all hide something from the others. So there is something lurking here which goes beyond mere mathematics, physics, geometry. In general, there is something wrong with bachelors in a properly ordered society.

He makes no demands on us. For the time being, at any rate. But, on the other hand, what does he give us? What is his contribution? In what sense can he be considered one of us? What does the community receive from him? What, in fact, keeps him here?

To be sure, mathematical infinity is a respectable subject. But in these times and in this place, what can it give us, what can it offer us?

It needs further reflection.

Perhaps a little consultation.

Now it's time for the news.

40

Ernst had an only son, a shiftless, withdrawn lad named Yotam.

From his childhood on the boy had suffered from weak nerves and short sight. Over and over again nurses and teachers had had to rescue him from the attacks of other children, who enjoyed tormenting and humiliating him in every possible way, both with words and with mischievous pranks. And when the boys left him alone he always fell victim to the sharp-tongued girls, who encircled him with scornful sniggers. Until he surrendered and burst into tears. And then the same girls who loved to reduce him to tears also loved to wipe away his tears with a great show of affection and genuine pity. Yotam was easily comforted, and that was the sign for a new round to begin.

Yotam gaped at the world through thick-lensed spectacles. Half a dozen times a day his weak fingers would let fall and shatter glasses, plates, records, vases, his spectacles, because his grip was feeble.

As if he refused to believe in the substantiality of objects.

Ever since the age of ten Yotam had never for a moment ceased to dream of a great power of domination which would be bestowed on him by virtue of his suffering. This power would force them all to kneel at his feet, to grovel and beg for mercy, pardon, compassion. Then his time would come to demonstrate to them, to the boys and especially to the girls, that he was not vindictive. On the contrary. His love would be given to all. To boys and girls alike. He would show them all a terrible, wonderful kindness, until their hearts filled with shame at everything they had done to him. What joy, what delight : to forgive and pardon day and night to his heart's content.

And so, alone for the whole of his childhood in the remote Galilean kibbutz, Yotam wandered among the white houses and neat gardens, the sheep pens, the cow sheds, the chicken runs, the stores, forgotten corners of the shady orchard, the heaps of hay in the barn, a village without cellars or attics. An emperor of China in shorts, with one leg rolled up higher than the other. Alexander the Great with little owl-like spectacles. A gracious king to all his subjects, in his daydreams he distributed to them all gold, marbles, pearls, caramels, and even key rings by the thousand. And in return he would inhale the savour of their love and excitement which would flow to him when the time came.

If in the meantime his subjects hit him, or the girls made fun of him, or plundered the coloured crayons from his pencil case, Yotam was not angry with them because they knew not who he was and what they were doing. And also because Ernst on his next trip would buy him a brand-new pencil case with twice as many colours. And Yotam had a secret lizard. Between two large cracked slabs of concrete behind the carpenter's shop lived a lizard and none of them knew about it, so they couldn't get up to any tricks with it. And none of them had a lizard. And they weren't going to have one either, no matter what new pranks they played on him.

Yotam cultivated certain odd habits. For instance, he would hop and skip along the paved paths in a way which those who saw him found amusing. In fact he was avoiding the cracks between the paving stones. Or he would press long and hard with his fingers on his eyelids, because when he pressed his eyeballs he saw a dizzying swirl of flashing lights. Only he did this in class, during lessons, and was made fun of for it.

He was always sniffling, love-lorn, and wretched.

Yet he was always eager to do good deeds.

Two or three years before, Yotam was called up for military service.

He was put behind a counter and taught to serve nicely, cookies, soft drinks, different brands of cigarettes, cellophane packages of peanuts.

Every evening he would assume a gentle, innocent smile and serve sweaty soldiers and strong, healthy girls whose khaki skirts stretched to bursting-point over their hips. He was forced to inhale the cigarette smoke of bossy-fat-bottomed officers, the smell of their breath, their coarse jokes told with sullen good humour, their air of rough, earthy virility.

Yotam stared blankly at them all through his thick bifocal lenses.

He half heard their inanities and obscenities, he saw with his own eyes how they were all dominated and desperately humiliated by a thousand base desires without being aware of them. A weary, blearing dullness covered everything with a coating of putrid decay.

One bright morning Yotam got up, scrubbed his teeth, washed his face and then washed it again, put on his glasses and decided that they were all, every single one of them, in need of urgent salvation. He did not exclude himself.

And so it occurred to him that he must get out of his uniform, go to Jerusalem, take the world by storm, wake everybody up, put a stop once and for all to war, to desires and to bad taste, and bring about peace everlasting.

To this end he began to set aside small sums from the proceeds of the soft drinks and cookies. Every night he distributed these sums to drivers, storekeepers, typists, and kitchen hands who vowed to him that they would surely follow him to Jerusalem, come what might.

So, one fine morning, Ernst's son Yotam absconded

from the camp through a small gap in the perimeter fence and started to march on Jerusalem. A quick-tempered rifleman by the name of Eliashar, Moshe and two corporals, Vilnay and Adorno, joined his expedition. There was also a short, stocky, thickset Hungarian girl soldier called Tehia Bamberger, a kitchen hand, a boy from the armoury, and two old labourers who were not in the army but made their living by keeping the perimeter weeded.

As they marched they came upon towns and settlements and villages, and wherever they came they sang and delighted the people, especially the children. While the cookies they had brought with them lasted they distributed them free to all the children. When they ran out of cookies they handed out some figs which they had found on a plot of wasteland by the wayside.

Halfway between Lydda and Ramla they were stopped by the military police. The only one to put up any resistance was Private Eliashar, Moshe, who fought with his teeth until he had to be tied up with ropes which in normal circumstances were used for securing loads on trucks. The other travellers all submitted quietly and without remonstrance.

Ernst's son Yotam was sentenced by court-martial to ninety days in the cells. He did away with himself several times in the hope of drawing attention to the terrible problems men failed to grapple with, such as loneliness, war, desires, and bad taste. But each time he was brought firmly back to his senses and the doctors informed him that his efforts were in vain, he must stop fighting, he was not mad, he was either pretending or he was an idiot.

Ernst, the Kibbutz Secretary, did not sit idly by. For days on end he travelled from place to place, enlisting the help of influential friends in the party and the Union, old comrades from the glorious 'thirties. His two middle-aged mistresses, Vera and Sara, did not disguise their fury: they maintained in unison that the real culprit was Elisha. And even though they were unable to explain or justify their suspicion, they stopped baking cookies for him. But after a while Ernst succeeded in bringing Yotam's case before a higher authority, and since the psychiatrists were now prepared to re-examine the case, Ernst's son Yotam was released from prison and from the army and sent home.

In next to no time the Kibbutz Committee had sent him to a course for youth instructors overseas, in the confident hope that in between lectures he would meet some sensitive girl and get over his trouble. Such cases had cropped up before, and some such solution had always been found.

And indeed Yotam did improve, although he did not change his mind about the need for urgent salvation. And meanwhile he was taught all the various tricks of the trade of a youth instructor, how to win adherents overseas, how to fan enthusiasm and how to channel it into the organized frameworks. He was even taught Spanish. Yotam's self-confidence grew. His acne disappeared. The Hungarian girl soldier Tehia Bamberger suddenly struck him as terribly small, stocky, and thickset.

Eventually Yotam was sent out to Argentina as an instructor. He lived in a commune along with several other young envoys from Israel, and took part in heated discussions which lasted into the early hours. After some months his eyes were opened and he saw the dazzling splendour of the wealthy villas on the outskirts, he saw stunning women, he saw life. And so he joined his maternal aunt, who had settled in Argentina and now exported canned beef all over the world in partnership with her daughter and two other elderly Russian émigrés.

But while Yotam was making progress toward a complete recovery and finding his niche in life, Ernst fell ill with a painful and incurable blood disease.

His grey eyes grew even greyer.

His mind was no longer exercised by Pomeranz's relations with kibbutz society. On the other hand, it sometimes happened in the evenings that the mathematical concept of infinity and the resultant paradoxes aroused his curiosity.

His eyebrow which was perpetually raised in astonishment—how could his interlocutor sink to such depths—now lowered itself to a level with its partner. His expression conveyed something resembling the rest of the hilltops to which Goethe's poem perhaps alluded.

41

He called on Pomeranz, too, occasionally, after the ten o'clock news. He sat with him and listened, and even put one or two questions.

Despite his illness, Ernst was still calm and composed; he showed no sign of alarm. He sat with his host and devoted himself to examining words and expressions, comparing them, weighing them, holding them up to the light, leaving them to soak for twenty-four hours, seeing what and checking how far.

The night which enfolded Ernst and his host, the early summer night which here in Galilee betrays a suffocating, simian quality, did not distract him from the even course he had followed all his life. Even the subject of which he was now trying to learn the rudiments did not lead him astray. He would return to his room before midnight, one of the women—sometimes both of them—would make him a glass of tea, hand him his pills, make up his bed, and in the meantime Ernst would type out a kind of résumé of what he had seen and heard, a kind of logbook or journal. He maintained his balanced style almost to the end, and subjected each word to an almost physical scrutiny before allowing it to take its place on the page. If there are one or two points, particularly in the final entries, where he seems to have lost his equilibrium somewhat, we must remember that he was seriously ill at the time, and was at the mercy of agonizing pain and bitter humiliation. And perhaps also apprehension.

First observation : If one reflects carefully on such concepts as gravity, inertia, or natural law, one simple conclusion emerges at once : the sciences employ metaphors and similes. A scientist would be thoroughly taken aback were his attention drawn to the literal meaning of such phrases as 'the earth's pull' or 'the attraction of opposites.' We are confronted by a choice : either-or.

Second observation : Mass. Energy. Electricity. Magnetic fields. On the other hand : Time. Space. Motion. And again : Will. Suffering. If all these have a 'meeting-point' or 'junction' – it is music. Without arriving at any conclusion we can report : from this there emerges a highly tempting hypothesis.

Third observation : Let us suppose for the moment that music is energy in a primary, more authentic form, and that it existed before all things and will outlive them all. Music, according to this line of reasoning, is metaenergy. And yet : it is interchangeable with mathematics. From here it is possible to arrive at 'thoughts like radar beams.' The possibility of trapping the will and suffering in a web of figures, on the supposition that what can be caught in notes can also be caught in numbers. Moreover, the system of reciprocal relations between the dimensions of time, space, and thought—and between these and energy, motion, and rhythm—all these have already been caught in music. If you possess the vital formula you will be able to translate everything into mathematics. Into formal quantitative relationships.

Fourth observation: We have before us, then, a musical scale. Time and will, electricity and image, space, magnetism, suffering, gravity, from now on they are all susceptible of being apprehended synoptically, all part of the same system, key, various modulations, rhythm. Transfiguration of time and matter. Resonant conjunction of the subjective and objective. Let us call this whole system 'mathemusics.'

Fifth observation: The mathematical theorem which 'operates' great galaxies and tiny particles alike, as well as the elements of life, is a theorem which can be grasped and expressed in music. The paradox of mathematical infinity is not 'solved' but actually disappears: in the musical system it is no longer a paradox, it is no longer in conflict with the fundamental logical forms. One possible practical implication is, for example, the conquest of gravity through the power of music. The dissolution of matter. Even the eradication of bearishness through the dance, to quote his own words. Music, therefore, is melodic mathematics, and whoever has the key is able (in principle) to transform matter into energy, energy into suffering, suffering into time, time into will, will into space, everything into everything else in any order whatever, as everything truly is before the mind breaks it down into different elements, some of which are completely distinct from the others. Music abolishes the distinction and once again everything becomes possible, provided you can master the universal music or – again to use words which are not my own —provided you can hear the song of the stars in their orbits and can reproduce it.

On the subject of magic et cetera Elisha is not prepared to waste a single word, and I am glad. Death is the bitterest modulation of all. Nothing more. Nothing less. A simple change of key. Sixth and last observation: I, Ernst Cohen, being of sound mind, hereby acknowledge the uncertainty of my five previous observations. I admit the possibility that they were written under the pressure of illness, pain, and fear. That they were all written not of my own free will but at the instigation of my present condition which has made me clutch at straws. That everything is a delusion which exists for a time only because the whole world, including the scientific world, is in desperate need of salvation, and therefore is prepared to accept for the time being any clever prophet, any novel formula because of its novelty, until some even more novel formula makes its appearance.

That nothing exists and nothing has ever existed. Neither he nor his equations and discoveries and signs, our after-dinner discussions, neither my son nor I myself, neither this hand nor the words it is writing. Nothing whatsoever. A dancing bear. A laughing fox. Nothing.

I, Ernst Cohen, at this moment, tonight, on the point of concluding this my last observation, hereby testify: here and now, with my very ears, I can hear the stars singing. There is no possible answer to the question, Is this in itself a sufficient proof that the stars are singing.

I may add that if I tried to grasp the melody, to repeat it, to reproduce it—there is no doubt that I should sing it out of tune.

Furthermore, it is late. And the night is cold.

42

Whenever Elisha Pomeranz recalled his wife, he could not remember her voice, but he could almost see her hair, the line of her neck and the curve of her shoulder, her gentle, dreamy fingers. And as from a great distance he could see the late afternoon light slowly fading around the belfry of St Stephen's Church, and the street lights coming on one by one along Jaroslaw Avenue, hesitantly, wrapped in a yellow haze, as though reluctant to mar the colour of the night. And the endless forests around the town of M——, in which there were quiet, decent things which a man could look for all his life and never find : bushes, stones, huts, squirrels, wild flowers, unbelievable wild flowers. There were foxes and hedgehogs, the song of the night breeze, the breath of empty paths.

He saw Stefa, slender and noble, silhouetted against the parapet of the bridge at night, smoking, facing toward the water the darkness the invisible forests, her back toward him. He himself standing apart a few paces behind her, not addressing her, not reminding her of his presence, not reminding her of the passing time, standing humbly, thoughtfully, almost desperately, he too smoking quietly. And just beneath their feet the river and the bridge, making no concession or allowance, ceaselessly flowing in two conflicting directions. The two crossed streams were love.

Stefa came home to the hills of Galilee on the morning of the day that Ernst died. The same morning, almost at the same time, Yotam too appeared, hurrying back from Argentina to take his leave of his father. Dying parents, Yotam thought, exercise a power over you that they have never had before. And when your father dies you will pick him up and carry him inside you all your life like an unborn child or a malignant growth, he will accompany you through all your rebellions, he will never again be angry or punish you but only laugh quietly inside you. All your life.

Naturally, Audrey too arrived in time : along with Jeff and Sandy and guitars, here as a volunteer, to work in the fields and in the evening to dream in the wood and at night make love. Audrey bronzed by the Red Sea sun, flashing revolutionary sparks, calling everything in the world by a new and more fitting name.

The day of Ernst's death was hot and sunny. Early summer, harsh merciless light, angry yellow stubblefields, the harvest almost over, three black crows seemingly nailed to the sewing-room roof. And the radio brought the grim news of concentrations of enemy troops on all four borders.

People furiously exchanged opinions and speculations. Interpreted the signs. Seized on circumstantial clues. Voiced desperate hopes.

Ernst had been sent home from the hospital the previous afternoon because instructions had been issued to discharge civilian patients, because his illness was incurable, and because Ernst himself had insisted on going home.

On account of the stifling heat his bed had been brought out on to the porch, and there the Secretary lay with his eyes open. He made a simple calculation and discovered that he had lived some twenty thousand days. He realized that for half this time, absurdly, he had tried to squander time, to speed it up to leave the first ten thousand days behind him, so as to reach the point where exciting things start happening as soon as possible. He had resented the irritating slowness of those first days. Whereas in the second half, in the last ten thousand days, he had subsided gradually into regret at the passing of all that had gone before : places, sounds, faces, smells, broken-down doors, paths he had never trodden, paths he would never tread again, nostalgia, yearnings, longings whose pain could only be driven away with other longings, he had become an addict, a slave, and the days in the second half had flashed past with vindictive, almost comic, speed. Like tiny figures in a silent film. And then this will-o'-the-wisp had appeared at the last moment, the peace of the mighty silent elements, the stars, the sea, the wind, the sands, darkness, music. Was there or was there not any substance in all this mirage. The powers of sober reflection which you have nurtured and trained for years and years abandon you now when you need them as you have never needed them before. Or perhaps they too were merely hidden traitors, making fun of you, pulling faces behind your back, fiends in disguise, demons and hobgoblins.

Ernst's features suddenly regained their long-lost expression of surprise and disappointment, the left eyebrow raised in discreet irony and veiled rebuke, 'How could you have done such a thing.'

There are various conflicting accounts of Ernst's death. Not long afterward war broke out, everything changed, minor matters were swept aside. According to one version, Ernst himself apparently decided to spare himself several days of agony and either took—or was given by his two mistresses acting on his instructions —an overdose of the morphine which had been prescribed to relieve his pain. And died within the hour. Others maintained the contrary, that he refused even to take the drugs which were essential to keep him alive for another week or two, that he terrorized the two women, dashed the medicine in their faces, threw the pills on the ground, and would not answer their questions with so much as a nod.

Whatever the truth of the matter, Ernst lay on his bed on the porch with the Lebanon Mountains behind him and the Syrian Heights to his left, and beyond the heights the legendary city of Damascus : its rivers Abana and Pharpar, myrrh and frankincense on the hidden side of the trenched and fortified hills. Ernst's two aged mistresses, little Vera, all shrivelled yet almost violently energetic, and tall, stooping Sara, with her thinning hair and her skill in making weird ceramic animals, sat with him all the time, almost day and night.

Occasionally one or other of them would take a damp handkerchief and soothe Ernst's grey hair, his temples, his mouth which still formed single carefully chosen words which pierced Yotam like nails as he sat nearby on a stool saying nothing and silently hating his own love for his dying father.

Sometimes Vera and Sara would get up nervously in unison and patrol the concrete path angrily together as far as the corner of the house and back again to the porch and the invalid's bedside. If Sara served Yotam a glass of tea, Vera would hasten to stroke his short-cropped hair. If Vera put a cushion behind his head, Sara wiped the perspiration from his forehead with the same damp handkerchief she had used to cool his father's brow. And whenever in an incautious moment the two women's eyes met, such meetings were always as brief as they could possibly be.

There is always a sense of something out of place in the death of a veteran pioneer in a well-organized, well-to-do kibbutz : as if some rule has been broken, the authority of one of the committees flouted, a discordant misdemeanour committed, the principle of seniority challenged, or even an enlightened ideal infringed. Something out of place, something that cannot be passed over in silence, or perhaps, on the contrary, something that cannot be mentioned at all, in case the general equilibrium is disturbed, or a dangerous precedent set.

And so a sensible, reasonable man, a broad-shouldered

man, a man possessed of an excellent sense of propor-
tion and clear-headedness which have never abandoned
him even in times of crisis, such a man writhes in
sweat and agony under a sheet on his bed on his porch
in broad daylight, utters a jumble of names, dates, and
places, for some reason passes complicated comments on
subjects of which he knows nothing, such as the Carib-
bean Sea or flights of cranes in autumn in another
country, reaches out to clasp his thin son Yotam in his
big tortured arms, tries to remember the name of an
old book, the name of a Czech nurse, and cannot; his
heavy body swelling with rage, he utters a vague protest,
gurgles, pushes away something that no one else can
see, throws a faint sentence to Yotam in his native
tongue, lets out a slight sob or belch, beats his brow
with a blind fist, and is gone.

43

Ernst died at ten past four in the afternoon. A little
earlier, toward the end of the morning, Stefa arrived at
the kibbutz. She was wearing a summer frock with an
abstract pattern of green lines. She was driven by the
man with bat's ears. He leapt out and opened the car
door for her with a waiter's alacrity and comically
broad gestures; then he took her arm lightly and told
his handsome young men to walk ahead and point
out any steps or obstacles in their way, and so, as if
to the accompaniment of a cheap bold march tune, the
little procession wended its way toward Elisha Pomeranz's room.

Twenty-five paces from the door of the house all
the men halted. Brimming with tact, their tense stance
displaying their deep consideration and respect, they
left Stefa to cover the final stage of her journey alone

and undistracted. How pale she looked. Even her lips were white. She went inside and the door closed behind her.

The fair-haired young men would remain for a while; they had orders to survey the locality, or perhaps to count the mountains and hills and compile an index of valleys until the receipt of further instructions. As for their master, he weighed anchor and was away, a little man with monstrous ears in a big wide car. He hummed some Jewish ya-ba-bam to himself, thumped the steering-wheel a couple of times, and pondered for a while a serious tactical error of Rabbi Jacob Emden, and Rabbi Jonathan Eibeschutz's failure, to his dying day, to exploit his opponent's blunder. For once the little man did not say much, even to himself. All he said was: Nature reigns supreme on mountain, vale, and stream. *Gematcht. Geendikt.*

44

Powerful pent-up forces were accumulating hour by hour. War was brewing. A tense heat filled the air. A panting. A strange stillness. The sun-scorched corrugated-iron roofs radiated a white-hot hatred. A belated spring blazed over the hills and plains. Not a bird was to be seen. The unharvested corn rustled drily as if sensing smoke. No dark forests here, Stefa, to flee to. Only white light. No abandoned huts to hide in, no last-minute chance to found a Goethe Society. Everything is enclosed. Everything is open and dazzling. Another war, but no water, no darkness. Run-Jesus. It's just as the Ruthenian doctor foretold, and his one-armed organist friend. They foresaw it all.

The harvest was halted. Even the weeding of the

cotton fields ceased, because all the young reservists had to rejoin their units. The older women cleaned out the air-raid shelters and picked flowers for wreaths for Ernst's funeral, which was to take place the next day. Elderly members, some of them shrivel-skulled like the ancient revolutionaries who ravished Stefa in Krasnoyarsk, others heavy-jawed and stubborn, their gnarled features expressing an almost prophetic rage, were summoned for emergency tasks. They pushed loaded handcarts from place to place, sorted cans of food, distributed candles and paraffin lamps, made up packages of cookies, filled water containers.

Even Ernst's two mistresses, despite their bereavement, were put to work crisscrossing windows with strips of gummed paper. Young Yotam, confused and frantic, volunteered to help dig pits and trenches. He was in a turmoil of indecision, because he could not come to terms with war, with the digging, with his father's death, with beef-canning; his whole life suddenly struck him as hopelessly confused and contradictory. Furthermore, the spadework was too much for him. His hands developed painful blisters, and when the blisters burst, and the salt sweat trickled into the open sores, and the dust, and the filth, the pain was severe and Yotam bit his lip and fought back a tear. On the other hand, he was happy and proud to show his father how he could bear hardship and how far he had dug. His father laughed soundlessly and his teeth showed big and white and amazingly strong. The son redoubled his efforts, began to dig hysterically, scattered soil in all directions, attacked the hard earth with his spade in a blind rage, with rapid ineffectual strokes, flailing like a drowning man. Before long he had hit his own foot, bled a little, and calmed down. His wound was dressed, and he was sent to sit down in the shade of the trees. There he encountered Audrey, who was preparing first-aid kits and rolling bandages. He introduced himself, spoke, received an answer. Audrey changed his dressing and agreed with everything he said. The hours flew by, she was ready to dry his sweat with her hair; and he took her by the shoulders and raised her to her feet.

Since Yehuda Yatom's son Shaulik had been mobilized to command his tank unit, it was necessary to put Pomeranz in sole charge of the sheep. There was a knock on his door at six o'clock in the evening. His guest accompanied him to the sheep pens and it was after dark when they made their way back to the dining hall.

Supper was eaten by the light of paraffin lamps, because the electricity supply was cut off. Those of the older members who were not away in the army or on special guard duty on the perimeter, together with the women and children, discussed over their meal the developments that might be expected. There were some who held that the moment of crisis had already been reached and that from now on there would be a gradual relaxation of tension. Some refused to believe that the outside world would stand aloof from the course of events. Others analysed the news and interpreted the signs. And still others maintained that the worst was still to come.

Many of those who were silent were not listening to the discussions but were thinking of Ernst lying all alone in a black-draped coffin set on four chairs on the large veranda of the recreation hall. Thanks to the power cut the coffin now lay in total darkness. And the easterly breeze brought the sounds and smells of the night to ruffle the shroud and perhaps even remove it to examine the wood and the slight gaps between the boards. These forces, everyone knew, were not friendly; they were not on our side.

There were a few who openly pronounced Ernst's name, and wondered what he would have said this evening, in the light of the new situation. It was not easy to get used to Ernst's death. There were even some who could not touch their food. They simply drank tea.

After the meal they all returned to the various tasks they had undertaken. Pomeranz and his guest were requested to work through the night in the stores. There was not a soul, elderly invalids and nursing mothers included, who did not volunteer for special duties. And the night was so deep that even the silhouettes of the mountains to the east were swallowed up in the darkness, they all began frantically cleaning. There were no further preparations to be made, so they scrubbed the floor of the clinic, they sprinkled the basins in the shelters with powerful disinfectants, they brushed the mosquito screens in the dining-hall windows, they sprayed concentrated insecticides in the outhouses, and they swept the concrete paths.

Out of the dark night came the sound of engines and the usual prattle of frogs and chorus of crickets. The sound of the crickets seemed much more distinct, much louder and more pentrating than on previous nights.

In the course of the night efforts were made in various quarters to allay the threat of war. Heads of state passed urgent messages. Various sources spread rumours to prevent desperate reactions. There were threats, there were insistent pleas. Emanuel Zaicek appeared simultaneously in many different places; knowing no rest, clad in the bear's skin, with his staff in his hand and his knapsack on his back he crossed lands and seas and wherever he came he preached to the people. There were no young men among his hearers : some had been called to arms, others were drinking in taverns or sleeping in their beds. Women, old folk, and little children eyed him with deep suspicion, half-hearing his voice gently caressing its every word; some cast stones, other kindlier souls offered him alms and broth. The philosopher Sartre and his circle drew up and circulated a carefully worded Open Letter addressed to the Arabs and other men of good will, imploring them to show restraint. And the secretive little man who had just brought Stefa home to her own land hurried on to his new task without even pausing to visit his shabby bachelor rooms on the outskirts of Old Bat-Yam. Quick as lightning as dusk fell he took off in a military aircraft for Malta. There he sat in a hotel bar and talked till the early hours with three American representatives in civilian clothes. The Americans were very discreet, pleasant looking and well spoken, with fine manners and a precise sense of humour. The little man, for his part, treated them to an exaggerated display of politeness, and addressed them in a patient Talmudic sing-song which after an hour or two had the effect of slightly numbing their senses. He larded his speech with proverbs and pointed syllogisms, leavened it with rhymes and sayings, skipped from subject to subject, made jokes at his own expense, painted elaborate word-pictures, then suddenly declared that enough was enough – we may not see the wood for trees, but there's no smoke without a breeze, as any man of sense agrees.

At two o'clock in the morning they consented. And not because he had got the better of them in argument, but because they were all three suddenly, simultaneously, and totally convinced that that was indeed how matters stood, that was what had to be done, and there was no conceivable alternative. At three o'clock he took off again for home, and by seven o'clock the same morning he could be seen eating a leisurely breakfast of omelette, roll, salad, and yoghurt in a small milk bar in Ben-Yehuda Street in Tel-Aviv.

At about the same time in Baden-Baden, the brothers were gathering in the chapel of the Dominican friary. They offered up prayers for peace for all men, and all morning long they tolled the bell.

45

Yotam and Audrey, meanwhile, had decided that words were not enough. They resolved that it was their duty to set out that very night on foot for the mountains over the border. There they would try with all their might and main to meet, to talk, to explain, to persuade, to extinguish with the right words the flame of blind hatred. Not that they had any confidence in the success of their experiment, but they both shared a feeling that there was nothing else in the world to compare to it, even if it failed, and that the almost certain defeat they faced would be far more glorious than all the magnificent victories of which the history books are full. The night was cold, and Yotam remembered to take a sweater each for Audrey and himself, so that they would not freeze to death on the way. How beautiful Audrey looked, with a man's sweater tied round her neck, bewitchingly long and slender, such a fragile body and such a firm resolve, she was gentle but determined, radiating love and fury, with a tiny gap between her two front teeth, and her perfect, innocent breasts sharing freely in her every movement. One of her sandal straps was broken and she had secured it with hairpins and a bit of yellow string. She was all aflame and heaving, and the orphan would have followed her to the ends of the earth, down the slopes, through the thistles in the wadi, with desperate devotion and steep longing, gasping, led on a halter, fighting back the song surging in his blood, repressing the mad urge to throw away his shoes and run barefoot after her, run singing, run healing and saving.

The fair-haired young men who had orders to remain until further notice observed the pair of them slipping

away into the wadi. They whispered a brief question into
the mouthpiece of their radio and received from far
away an unexpected answer. They remained motionless,
sniffing the cold dark air.

Over all, as always, the bear's glass eyes looked down.

Ernst's lips twisted in the darkness into an expression
of faint disgust, as if a voice had suddenly said : Ernst,
come forth.

46

At nine o'clock in the evening hundreds of Syrian guns
began firing shells at the kibbutz, at Galilee, and at all
the valleys among the hills and below them. Arcs of
horror flashed across the sky, rolls of thunder chased
one another, the Sea of Galilee was lit up, and from time
to time a column of wounded water rose fruitlessly in
a demented spasm and was shattered into foamy drop-
lets that also surrendered and fell back into the lake.
They stood side by side leaning on the window ledge
of his room in the dark, and he was able to tell her
how far off down the forest slopes, where the undergrowth lapped at the river, the German engineers had
dynamited all the railway bridges, while he had watched
from his hiding-place in the woodcutter's hut. And how
because of the murky distance and the thickness of the
air there had been a delay, a hesitation almost, between
the flash of each explosion and the low rumble of
thunder, and how this delay, momentary though it
was, had given an almost comical appearance to the
whole spectacle, so that he in his hideout had been
assailed by doubts. And how, indeed, a few days later,
the German engineers had reappeared, on receipt of
fresh orders, and begun hastily and furiously to rebuild
everything as it had been before, and how unreal all

events and places were. And since he had begun and she had not interrupted him, he made an effort and told her more, and she too disclosed one or two memories, and later when the shelling became more savage, and aged firefighters appeared outside in the light of the blaze and tried to stave off disaster, they managed perhaps to reach a measure of agreement, a certain tentative conclusion, before they too went outside. Beautiful, proud Stefa, whom from her youth on literary men had longed to touch with ideas, and the dreamy son of a watchmaker, whom she had chosen and preferred and believed in, and whose cheek she had yearned from a distance to touch with her hand and to see what would happen to her hand and whether the touch would alter the lines of his face. His natural powers of loneliness, which she longed to touch and be touched by, even at the cost of her life. At the cost of ascending in flames. Even death, if she might not bear his son.

They went out and passed among the shadows and the reflected flames and strolled beyond the deserted avenue, and their shoulders met and touched.

(As for the story of the war, the full story in all its details, it still remains to be sung and loudly proclaimed; Gershon Kumin, the mighty old poet, has yet to celebrate all its marvels, in the manner of the hymns of the new kingdom of Poland in the Aegean Islands. And there will be no shortage of drums and bugles, no lack of exultant bliss.) Furious shells continued to burst blindly on the kibbutz, like backward pupils who had rebelled against mathematics and hidden music and now vented their pent-up rage on the beleaguered island of orderliness. Preying talons caressed red-tiled roofs to smithereens, decapitated trees, pulverized outhouses, ripped the bull to shreds. It was all loud and hoarse and coarse without any rhythm or style, with loud howls and strident shrieks and blasts

of fiery breath. Jets of dust and savage eddies. Violent
bestial lust, salvo upon salvo upon salvo.

The whole mad orgy, which may have echoed dim and
menacing in the distance, was merely clumsy and banal.
A noisy performance, tedious, familiar, overplayed,
exaggerated, excessive : saturated with pork fat.

47

And so it came about that, an hour or so after midnight,
Elisha and Stefa Pomeranz arrived at the big lawn in
front of the recreation hall.

They stood at the edge of the lawn and watched the
arcs of shells and flames all around. There was fire
reflected in the darkened windows of the recreation
hall. And Ernst's coffin lay long and dark on its four
wooden chairs. A coil of rope lay in the corner.

Meanwhile, among the mountain ravines, Yotam and
Audrey were groping their way under the shrieking
dome of fire. They wound their way safely past fences,
minefields, and trip wires. Had they been given the
power of levitation, or was there no power, no levitation,
but the following wind of their own enthusiasm clearing
the way ahead?

On the edge of the lawn they stood side by side in
the darkness, while overhead the shells flashed and
above the shells the night with its crickets and farther
still were the stars in their regular nightly stations.

A man and a woman, both of them thin, neither of
them young, almost insubstantial in the flickering darkness which shone that night over Galilee, the mouth
organ in her white hand, then in his hand as he played.

The man played. The music mingled with the darkness. A small crack began to show at their feet, like
the cracks that appear in heavy earth at the end of

summer. A narrow, dry, serpentine chink, then more music, and it was no longer dry, now a warm moist slit, and still more music. The darkness was all-pervading. The topmost crust of earth yielded in the moist blindness with rippling spasms at the wetness of the warm virginal lips and they were slowly drawn inside. For a moment longer the slit quivered, then relaxed and enfolded them in a silent embrace of unbelievable tenderness. The melody died away. The lawn healed over. The stars shone unaltered. Toward dawn the artillery fire was resumed. But, as is well known, the mountain plateau was swiftly stormed and all its guns were silenced. This war was a short one.

Many refuse to believe. They neither saw nor heard. Others believe it all. Some even attribute to that patch of lawn powers of healing or powers of atonement and purification.

Summer after summer a savage sun blazes. In the winter the rain beats down and the wind lashes the pine trees. Yotam and Audrey roam from town to town and from land to land, testing the power of words, always supposing that they are not exporting canned beef. There is no possible end to the unfathomable soughing of the evening breeze in the pines in the late autumn. Occasionally six or seven men and women gather at the spot at dusk and celebrate a ritual; they produce a low, long-drawn-out melody.

But by that hour of the evening the bright lights are on in the recreation hall. And from inside the brightly lit hall comes the cheerful blare of a different music.

1972